The
Life
of
Zerah

To get in touch with the publisher, please email us at: hello@mosaicstreetpress.com
To get in touch with the author, please email her at: jordanamayim@yahoo.com

Exquisite Book Designer: Sophia Glock; sophiadraws.com
Exquisite Editor: Joy Tibbs; joyediting@gmail.com
Exquisite Mosaic Street Press Logo Designer: ÂGrizon

Publisher's Cataloging-in-Publication data

Names: Mayim, Jordana Chana, author.
Title: The Life of Zerah / written and illustrated by Jordana Chana Mayim
Description: Narberth, PA: Mosaic Street Press, LLC., 2018.
Identifiers: ISBN 978-1-948267-04-5 (Hardcover) | | 978-1-948267-02-1 (pbk.) | 978-1-948267-03-8 (mobipocket) | 978-1-948267-05- 2 (epub) | 978-1-948267-06-9 (Adobe PDF) | LCCN 2018936333
Subjects: LCSH Seeds--Fiction. | Trees--Fiction. | Social problems--Fiction. | Kindness--Fiction. | Self-realization--Fiction. | Spirituality--Fiction. | Family--Fiction. | Friendship--Fiction. |
Allegorical fiction. | BISAC FICTION / Visionary & Metaphysical
Classification: PS3613.A9563 L54 2018 | DDC 813.6--dc23

First Edition

The Life of Zerah

Written and Illustrated

by

Jordana Chana Mayim

MOSAIC
STREET
PRESS

Dedicated to

a seed named Zerah

the Wind that blew him into my life

all the exquisite grains of sand, twigs, blades of grass,
ants, and birds
I have been blessed to meet

the beautiful dream

and the hope that we can fulfill it

IT WAS A WINDY day. Leaves shared space in the sky with birds. Blades of grass rippled like a sea. The sun's light shone, then disappeared, then shone again, perpetually affected by the journey of the clouds.

Meanwhile, I sat upon a park bench, weeping. My life was not what I had dreamed it would be. I had not become who I wanted to be. And the world was full of pain, injustice, and broken hearts. I didn't know how to change any of these things.

I spoke one word to the Wind, "How?"

In the next instant, a seed landed in my lap and said to me, "I also used to ask that question. Do you want to know how I found the answer?"

I nodded. It was then that a seed named Zerah told me his story.

There was once a seed named Zerah.

Zerah was a little seed growing on a Great Tree.

ZERAH

But even though he was a little seed, Zerah had a big dream for his life. He would become a Great Tree. He knew exactly how it would happen, for he had planned it all with the help of his Great Tree.

When the first snowflake fell, along would come the Wind to carry Zerah to a field. Once in a field—preferably an empty one that would afford him all the space he needed to grow in greatness—Zerah would find the perfect spot to root himself: a soft, moist, reddish-brown patch of earth that would immediately feel like home.

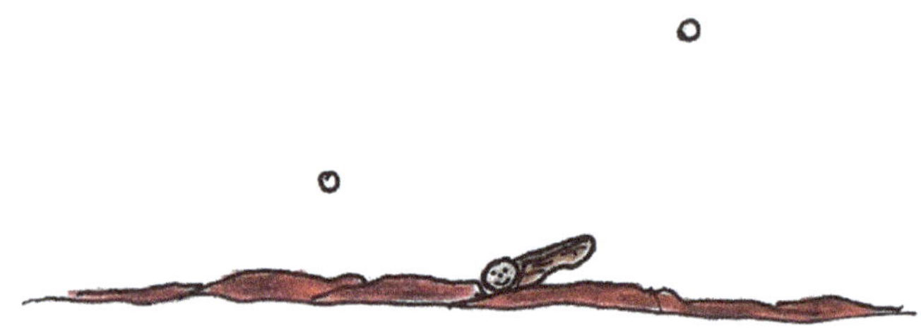

Then the snow would start to fall harder.

By the time the snow covered the ground, Zerah would be buried deep beneath it, already growing roots.

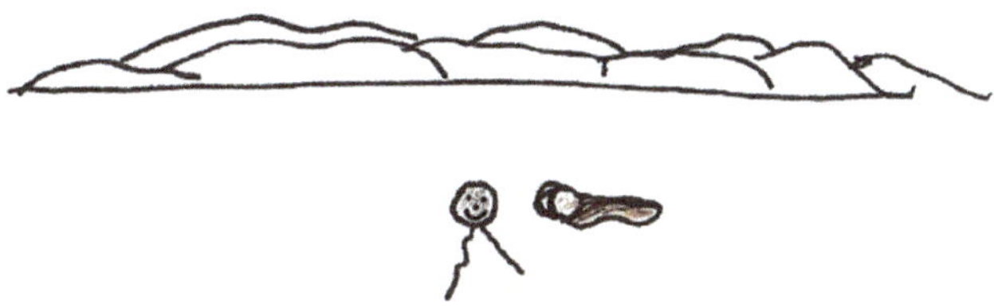

By the time the snow melted, Zerah would have a firm grip on the soil and a clear view of the sky.

And by the time the rainy season had come and gone, and the sunny season had left and returned—once, twice, perhaps three times—Zerah would be a Great Tree, just like the one that had given him life. And once Zerah was a Great Tree, oh, how he would change! How his *life* would change!

First of all, he would have a trunk: a big, thick one in shades of red and brown with streaks of black, amber, and gold. Next, he would have strong, secure branches and plenty of them at that; all tall enough to know the sky as intimately as the clouds. Hundreds of leaves would grow on his branches: green and tender in the spring; red and wise in the fall. Delicious fruit—round, orange, sweet, and succulent—would grow between the leaves, and exquisite flowers—soft, fragrant, and in the colors of the sunrise—would bloom beside the fruit. Last, but most certainly not least, Zerah would have seeds of his own.

But, oh, this was only the beginning! Once Zerah *had* these wondrous things, he would *do* wondrous things! Zerah was going to change the world! His trunk would provide ants with a stable place to crawl during the day, and his branches would give birds a comfortable place to sleep at night. His leaves would shelter spiders weaving their webs, and caterpillars spinning their cocoons. Mice, dogs, and humans would find a place to cool off and rest in the shade his leaves and branches provided. With his fruit he would feed hungry bellies and quench thirsty mouths, and with his flowers—indeed, with his entire self—he would nourish parched souls, adding as much beauty to the earth as the stars did to the sky; a beauty so all-encompassing that, even on rainy days and cloudy nights, no one would ever be without light. Through his seeds he would create trees as numerous as the blades of grass in a field. These trees would live on long, long after he was gone. And when they died, Zerah's name and the memory of his great accomplishments would endure, passed on from tree to seed to tree forever.

Yes, Zerah could see many things in his future, but the most crucial one was this: by the time he had housed the homeless, given rest to the tired, satiated the hungry, added beauty to the world, and ensured himself of eternal life, Zerah would be important, useful, special, happy, and, most of all, loved. Yes, Zerah would be all these things once he became a Great Tree instead of what he believed he was now: an insignificant, useless, ordinary, and empty little seed.

A SINGLE SNOWFLAKE fell to the ground beneath Zerah, disappearing into the soil almost as though it had never been. But it had been. Even if no one else had seen it, Zerah had. He knew what the first snowflake meant.

"The Wind is coming for me!" he shouted with glee. "I'm going to become a Great Tree!"

He felt his heart fill with a love that was not yet, but would be.

Zerah held back his tears as he said goodbye to his Great Tree, and his trunk, branches, leaves, fruit, flowers, and other seeds. But when Zerah turned toward the seed growing next to him, his best friend, Semeeya, a single tear from each eye led two thin, silent processions of drops to the ground. They disappeared into the earth like the snowflake before them, almost as though they had never been.

But they had been, and even if no one else had seen them, Semeeya had.

"I'll miss you," she said, as her own tears followed his into the soil.

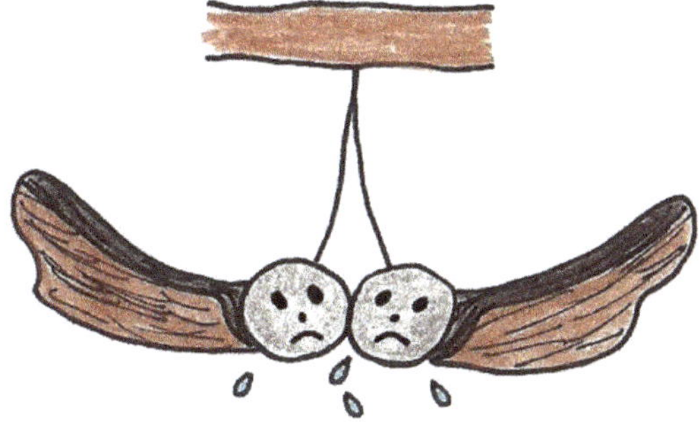

Soon a tiny puddle had formed, from which two parched ants quenched their thirst.

"I'll miss you too," Zerah said.

"I hope to see you again one day," sniffed Semeeya.

"Of course you'll see me again!" exclaimed Zerah.

Zerah looked far beyond Semeeya into the future, and he couldn't help but smile. He had once overheard two birds speaking about the world. They had said that it was a giant sphere made of green and blue. He didn't know what the blue was, but he knew that he would grow so great that no matter where anyone or anything was on that sphere, they would see him!

As Zerah's gaze shifted from the future back to the present, he said to Semeeya, "Come with me."

"What?" she asked.

"Come with me! You're ready to become a Great Tree, aren't you? It'll be fun! We'll keep each other company underground. And if either of us gets bored waiting for the snow to melt, we'll have each other to talk to."

Zerah looked at Semeeya, waiting hopefully for her reply.

He didn't have to wait long. A smile brightened her face and the promise of constant, tender companionship dried her tears. "And if either of us gets discouraged waiting for the sun to dry the rain, we'll have each other to cheer ourselves up!"

Zerah's smile shined as brightly as Semeeya's.

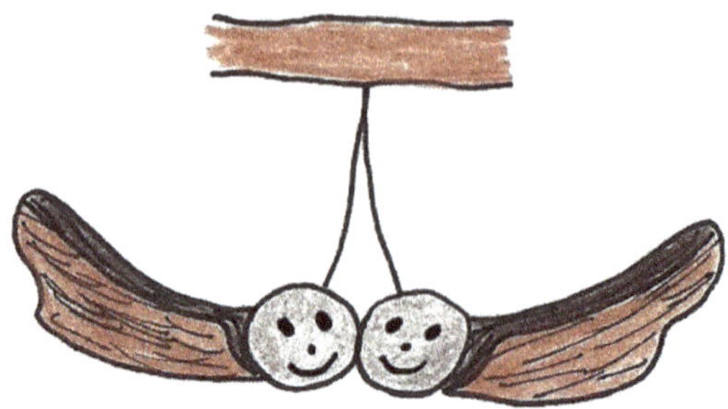

Then they kissed their Great Tree goodbye, and he sent them off into the world just as the Wind gently caught hold of them.

The Wind carried them to a field that was empty of other trees.

It dropped Semeeya onto a moist patch of earth surrounded by several blades of grass. She immediately settled into the soft ground.

Zerah was deposited onto a brownish-red lump of soil, far enough away from Semeeya that her roots wouldn't interfere with his, yet close enough that her voice would reach him through the patter of raindrops, the chatter of spiders, and the footfall of ants.

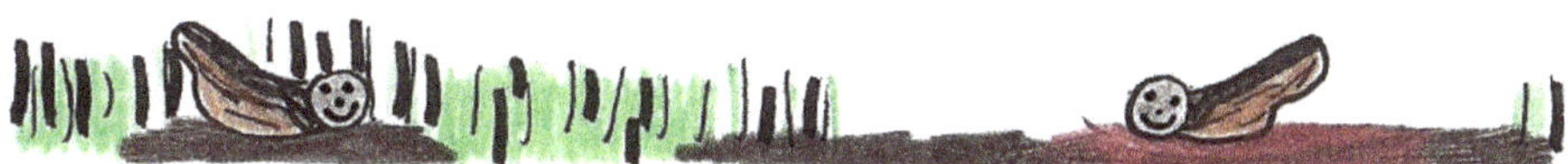

The Wind shifted Zerah tenderly from side to side. Just as he was getting comfortable, the Wind grew a little stronger. It picked him up and carried him further away from Semeeya, dropping him onto a yellowish-green tuft of moss.

Well, thought Zerah, *we'll have to shout to make ourselves heard. But at least here I'll have even more space to gr—*

The Wind grew stronger again. Before he knew what was happening, Zerah was no longer on the ground, or anywhere even close to it, but high up in the sky.

"Zerah!" he heard Semeeya's voice cry out from behind him.

"Semeeya!" Zerah yelled, hoping the Wind would carry the sound of his voice to her, even as it carried his body away.

Specks of dust whirled beside him and clouds could not keep pace with him. The quiet hum he had often heard when the Wind was close by abandoned its melody and was now a tuneless moan.

Zerah screamed, "Wind! Put me down!"

The Wind blew harder. The moan grew louder.

Zerah squeezed his eyes shut. The view of the distant fields below, along with the rapid pace at which he was passing over them, was beginning to make him feel dizzy, and more than a little queasy.

Zerah cried out again, "Wind! Didn't you hear me? *Put. Me. Down!*"

But the Wind did not put Zerah down. Perhaps the Wind didn't hear or understand him. Or maybe it heard and understood everything Zerah said but had plans of its own for him. Or perhaps, unlike Zerah, the Wind had no plans at all. Whatever the reason, the Wind carried Zerah a very great distance before it eventually put him down.

When Zerah felt the ground beneath him, he slowly opened his eyes, focused his vision, and looked around. There was no soil or blades of grass; no trees, animals, humans, or insects. Instead, there was something grainy and tan-colored to his left. And something grainy and tan-colored to his right. Before him, behind him, and beneath him was something grainy and tan.

Then Zerah looked above him and saw the vast blue sky, and his heart began to ache. Was this the same sky his future trunk, branches, leaves, fruit, flowers, and seeds were supposed to reach towards and eventually touch? Now the sky would be forever out of his reach; a home eternally shared with the sun, moon, and stars, but not with him. Zerah didn't know where he was, but he knew this much: without soil, he couldn't root himself.

I guess I will never be important or useful or special or happy or loved, because I will never become a Great Tree, thought Zerah. *I will never become anything. I will remain what I already am: nothing.*

Tears fell silently from his eyes, and pain pushed all remaining hope to the bottom of his heart, hushing it to sleep. Zerah closed his eyes and fell asleep in turn.

MANY DAYS LATER, Zerah awoke to find a single grain of the grainy tan something staring at him.

"Are you OK?" she asked, her eyes wide.

Blurry-eyed, Zerah blinked and looked around him, uncertain as to whether this was a strange dream from which he would soon awaken. But this was not the case.

The grainy tan something spoke again. "I first heard you crying many, many days ago. I tried to talk to you, but you didn't hear me. Then you fell asleep. Are you OK?"

A great sob broke free from Zerah's lips, despite his attempt to contain it. "No, I am *not* OK. I'm in a...in a...in a... Where *am* I?"

"In a desert."

"What is that?" asked Zerah.

"That is this!" grinned the grainy tan something.

Zerah rolled his eyes. "Ah, that clears up everything! And who are you?"

"I am a grain of sand," the Grain of Sand replied.

"And what is that?"

"That is me!" answered the Grain of Sand happily.

Zerah looked the Grain of Sand over. He wondered what she had and did that made her so happy. But as he surveyed all the other grains of sand lying around him in the desert, he felt certain that she had what they all had, and did what they were all doing, which is to say, nothing.

"Who are *you*?" the Grain of Sand asked Zerah.

Zerah spoke through uneven breaths, but his words were as stable as rocks. "I am Zerah, a seed who is *not* OK! I'm in a *desert* when I *should* be in a *field*. I'm above ground *doing nothing* when I *should* be beneath it, *growing roots*. I'm *pouring out sweat* when the rain *should* be *pouring on me*. I will never grow here. *Never*." The corners of Zerah's mouth sunk down towards the earth.

The Grain of Sand tried to raise them up.

"Dear Zerah, it is not true that you are doing nothing. You are talking to me! And to offer someone your ear, your time, and a space inside your life is something very great indeed! Who's to say what you should be doing, anyway? *You* are to say. So if you say that you should be talking to me, then you will start to feel better, for you are doing what you should be doing.

"Zerah, you have only just arrived in the desert, so you don't yet know what it's like here. Although it is not a field, there *is* rain here. Even in the desert, it sometimes rains. There are seeds that have become trees here. It may not be easy, but I don't think it is ever easy, even for a seed in a field. I think there is always a bit of a struggle, no matter who you are or where you are. I think you can root yourself anywhere if you truly want to."

Annoyance and disbelief momentarily took the place of Zerah's pain. He stared at the Grain of Sand in shock.

Is she crazy? How can she think that simply talking to her is as valuable as feeding the world? Or that it is up to me to decide what I should do? Seeds should become trees. That is what all seeds do! Doesn't the Grain of Sand know that? Doesn't she know that life decides the "shoulds," not those living it? But the most ridiculous—the worst—of all the things the Grain of Sand has said is that I can root myself here, in the desert.

That the desert needed more beauty was certainly true. Up until his arrival there, Zerah had never understood what *ugly* meant. A butterfly fluttering beside him while he was still growing on his Great Tree had once used the word, followed by a definition that had made no sense to Zerah: "Ugly is a caterpillar. Ugly is the opposite of beautiful."

Zerah had always considered caterpillars to be as beautiful as butterflies.

And so he couldn't imagine what the opposite of beauty might be. But right there, in the desert, Zerah didn't have to imagine. He knew.

The desert must be the ugliest place in the world! he thought. Yet regardless of how much beauty he could offer the desert, he wondered how he could ever truly become who he wanted to be without animals, humans, and insects. *Is a Great Tree truly great*

"Maybe you're right," Zerah conceded. "Maybe I *can* root myself anywhere. But I don't *want* to just root myself anywhere. I want to root myself in a *field*!"

The Grain of Sand spoke tenderly to Zerah. "I think I understand. If one day I opened my eyes to find myself far from everyone and everything I knew—in a field, for example—I would also be sad. I understand that you don't want to be here, but that doesn't change the fact that you are here right now. Just because you don't want to root yourself here, that doesn't mean that you cannot still grow here. You can grow anywhere."

Zerah sighed in exasperation. He was growing, all right. Growing tired of the Grain of Sand!

"Look, you don't understand. But how could you? A grain of sand can live in a field or in a desert. What's the difference? No matter where you are, you're still just a grain of sand. You have no purpose in life. All you do is lie on the ground. But a seed living in a desert or in a field? Those are two very different things. If I rooted myself here, my branches would go unlived in, my shade unused, my fruit uneaten, and my seeds unable to reach their potential. Don't you see?"

The Grain of Sand looked at Zerah through the tears that were clouding her eyes. The hurt in her heart drained her voice of the happiness that had filled it just moments earlier. "What I see is how unstable your branches, how partial your shade, how bitter your fruit, and how unhappy your seeds would be. You would offer these to the world, yet you would offer them without love."

Zerah shook his head. *The Grain of Sand truly understands nothing! Of course I will offer such things without love, at least at first. Until I have such things and can offer them, where will the love come from?*

"Listen," Zerah said to the Grain of Sand, deciding to give her one last chance to help him. "If you could just tell me how to get to a field, then one day, when I am a Great Tree, I will tell everyone about you: the Grain of Sand that helped me."

Now it was the Grain of Sand's turn to be annoyed.

"Tell you how to get to a field?" she asked incredulously. "But how could I do that? I'm just a grain of sand. I have no purpose in life. All I do is lie on the ground. I don't help seeds get to fields. I wonder what the rain's purpose is. Only to nourish you, perhaps? Maybe the ground exists purely to give you a place to root yourself? And humans were born solely to admire you?"

Zerah looked at the Grain of Sand, stunned. He didn't know what to say, nor did he have time to think of anything. Along came the slightest breeze and, in an instant, the Grain of Sand was carried away.

"Wait!" Zerah cried out. "Come back, Grain of Sand! Please! Tell me how to get to a field! I'm sorry… I didn't mean what I said… I was just upset… I was angry… I wasn't ready to come to the desert… I wasn't ready for my plans to be changed!"

"No one ever is," spoke the Desert.

And then there was silence.

Zerah was silent as well. He stared off into the distance at the traceless path the vanished leave behind. Then he put his head down. His eyelids, heavy with the burden of trying to protect him from that which he didn't want to see, lowered. And so Zerah passed many of his first days in the desert: with his eyes closed to all that was around him.

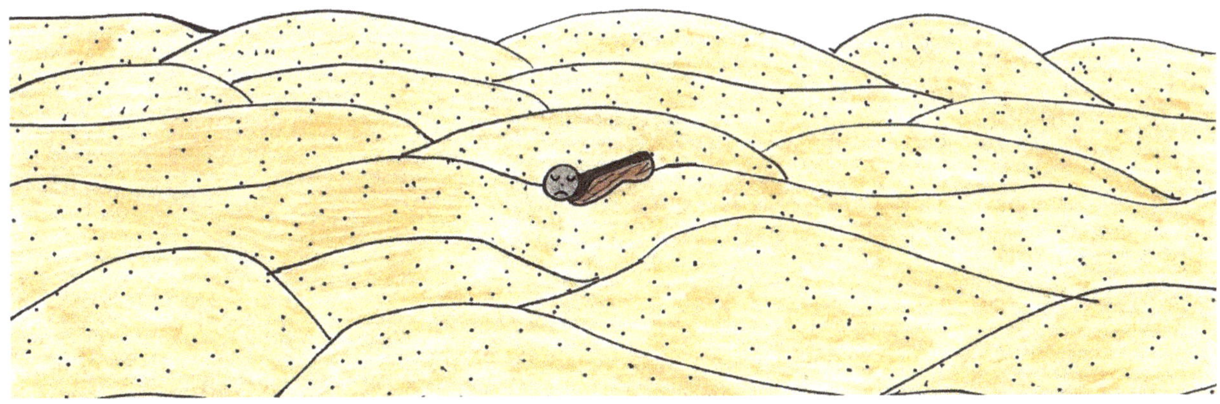

MANY SUNRISES CAME to kindle fire in the sky, and many sunsets returned to extinguish it. The moon waxed and waned, speaking of impermanence and telling old tales about the changelessness of change. Dust particles and grains of sand heard music in every whisper and sigh of the Wind. They surrendered to its touch, joining the ecstatic dance of the here and now. But for Zerah, it was as though there was no light, no music, no dance. There was simply moment after moment, each the same as the one before. He was rootless, trunkless, branchless, leafless, fruitless, flowerless, seedless, and loveless.

How do I get to a field so I can root myself and become a Great Tree? Zerah asked himself again and again. Then one day, the answer finally dawned on him, just as the sun did in the morning sky, and he saw the light.

Of course! I can ask another grain of sand. The desert's full of them. Isn't one grain of sand exactly the same as another?

Zerah turned to the grain of sand lying to his left, cleared his throat, and said, "Excuse me, Grain of Sand."

There was no answer.

Zerah faced the grain of sand to his right. "Ahem," he coughed as loudly as he could. "Grain of Sand?"

There was no answer.

Zerah looked straight ahead at the grain of sand before him and shouted,

"Annoying creature!" the Grain of Sand yelled back.

"Oh!" Feeling startled, Zerah began to stutter. "I d-didn't mean to sh-shout. I-I didn't know if you c-could hear me."

"Well of course I can hear you," replied the Grain of Sand miserably. "You're shouting. The whole desert can probably hear you. What do you want?"

"I-I," Zerah stuttered even more, "I w-w-anted to know if you c-c-could tell me how to g-get to a f-f-f-f-field?"

"Get to a *what?*" asked the Grain of Sand.

"To a f-field," repeated Zerah, making a concerted effort not to stutter, but not quite managing it.

"What is that?" asked the Grain of Sand, ever so slightly intrigued.

Zerah's eyes grew large. *This grain of sand doesn't know what a field is! Doesn't everyone know what a field is? How ignorant can he be? And if he doesn't know, how can he help me get to one? Unless, maybe, the Grain of Sand does indeed know what a field is, but simply calls it by another name, just like I sometimes call the Wind, the Breeze.*

Hmm... How do I describe a field?

Zerah thought and thought while the Grain of Sand stared and stared.

Finally, Zerah triumphantly declared, "A field is a place where a tree grows."

"What's a tree?" asked the Grain of Sand.

Zerah's mouth dropped open. *Not knowing what a field is, that's bad enough, but not knowing what a tree is... How empty the Grain of Sand's life must be! How is it possible?*

Was the First Grain of Sand mistaken, or a liar? Are there really trees in the desert?

"You must be joking!" Zerah said in disbelief.

"Do I sound like I'm joking?" asked the Grain of Sand soberly.

"No," Zerah gulped. He started to explain, "A tree is—" and then he stopped. He had been about to say, "the most important thing in the world," but then he thought better of it. He didn't want to upset this grain of sand as he had the first. This grain of sand was already annoyed. Zerah shivered at the thought of annoying him further.

No wonder these grains of sand are so touchy! Unlike me, they cannot become anything. They are stuck with being who they already are forever.

Suddenly, Zerah knew how to describe a tree.

"A tree is what I will become!" Zerah beamed. "Tall and wide and strong!"

The Grain of Sand snorted. "And how will you become that?"

"Well, first I will be carried to a soft, moist, reddish-brown patch of earth by the Wind—"

Laughter, loud and harsh, cut Zerah off. The Grain of Sand's voice boomed out again and again, leaving Zerah no space to ask him what was so funny.

When the Grain of Sand's laughter finally abated, he said, "You will be carried to a soft, moist reddish-brown patch of earth by the Wind. Really? Who do you think you are?"

Zerah's voice rang out with the certainty of a chorus of birds announcing the dawn. "I am Zerah, a seed who will become a Great Tree in a field!"

"Well, Zerah," the Grain of Sand continued condescendingly, "if you're depending upon the Wind to become a Great Tree, I'd make a plan to become something else. Or become nothing and remain as you are. I mean—and please, correct me if I'm wrong—but wasn't it the Wind that brought you *here?*"

Zerah swallowed. "Yes," he said, his voice shrunken to the size of a speck of dust.

"Well then," said the Grain of Sand, his tone cruel. "Why are you asking me how to get to a field? You already know the answer. Only, it's not an answer you want to hear, because now you know you're at the mercy of the Wind. The only problem is, the Wind is merciless."

A tear fell from Zerah's eye.

The Grain of Sand's voice shed its harshness at the sight, and pity took its place. "Look, Zerah, do you think you're the first one to be blown here by the Wind? Do you think you're the first one to speak to me of places I've never been and things I don't know? Do you think you're the only one with dreams? I once dreamed of leaving the desert, travelling to a place called the ocean, and becoming a grain of sand on her floor. But I have neither legs like an ant, nor wings like a bird. I cannot even slither like a snake. I am totally dependent upon the Wind to take me places, but the Wind takes me nowhere, except from one part of the desert to another. Tell me, legless, wingless seed, how do you think you can leave the desert, except by the graciousness of the Wind? Yet it was that very *graciousness* that brought you here."

The Grain of Sand looked around the desert, then back at Zerah. "Do you know what justice is, Zerah?"

Zerah shook his head.

"Neither does the Wind. Justice means fairness. Fairness means if you do good things, good things happen to you. And if you do bad things, you face consequences. That means you cannot live the same way after the hurt you've caused as before it. Depending upon how much hurt you've caused, some creatures believe you should not even continue living. But no matter how much hurt the Wind causes, it blows the same today as it did yesterday and as it will tomorrow. And no matter how much good you do, the Wind will still blow you about. Don't you see, Zerah? It doesn't matter what you become. You will always remain what you are: dependent on the Wind."

With that, the Grain of Sand shed a single tear, rolled over in a breeze and went to sleep.

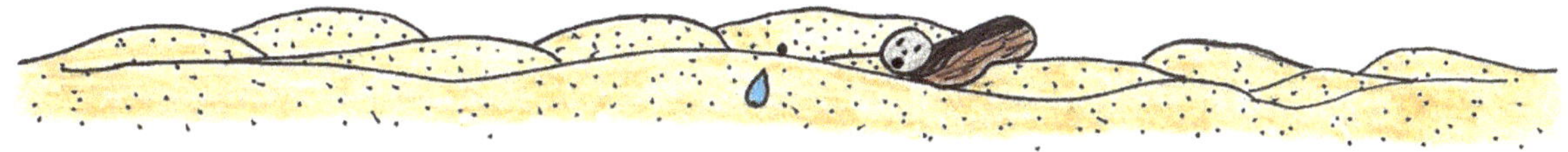

Zerah watched the Second Grain of Sand's tear seep between the other grains of sand. He imagined what it would be like to feel that same moistness surrounding him, only in his case from drops of rain and in the comforting embrace of specks of soil. The journey in his mind back and forth between where he was and where he wished to be soon exhausted him. As he entered slumber once more, he hoped that a reprieve from his pain would accompany it at long last.

SLEEP CAME, BUT rest did not. The Second Grain of Sand's words had journeyed from Zerah's ears to his heart, where they found the unspoken version of themselves. Thoughts that had once whispered to Zerah, *The Wind doesn't care what happens to you,* now shouted. They gathered evidence. They offered nothing of comfort to replace the hope they had taken. Fear and despair filled up his heart, and the Wind's constant presence in the desert made those feelings more difficult to bear.

For a very long time there had been no Wind around Zerah except for the slightest breeze, which was only strong enough to shift a grain of sand or two a little to the left, or a little to the right. Fierce windstorms had been roaring away in the distance, but Zerah had managed to ignore them.

The distance between Zerah and the Wind was now dwindling. He watched as grains of sand and specks of dust flew in circles like birds. He saw that the dragonflies moved more slowly when the Wind was before them, and faster when it was behind them. He noticed that the butterflies' wings fluttered even when they were not in flight. Then Zerah began to feel the Wind on his own body, shifting him a little to the left, then a little to the right.

Before the Wind grew strong enough to pick him up and drop him somewhere even worse than the desert, Zerah buried himself as quickly and as deeply as he could beneath the grains of sand. Though the thought of being trapped in the desert forever and either becoming a tree there or simply remaining nothing was painful for Zerah, it did not pain him as much as the prospect of leaving the desert with the same Wind that had brought him there.

Long before Zerah dropped from his Great Tree, he had spent many nights gazing at the tremendous distance between the branch on which he was growing and the very hard ground beneath it.

"Will it hurt when I drop?" Zerah had asked his Great Tree one day. "The distance is great, and I am small."

"Distance and size mean nothing to the Wind," his Great Tree had replied. "When it's time for you to drop, the Wind will carry you in its embrace to a field, where you will root yourself and become a Great Tree."

"A Great Tree just like you?" Zerah had asked. "With a huge trunk and lots of branches and leaves and fruit and flowers and seeds?"

His Great Tree had shed tears as a cloud releases a light drizzle after a storm: just a few small drops, barely visible. Then his eyes had gleamed as brightly as the sun, and his smile had radiated just as much warmth. "Of course! That, my dear seed, is why you were born: to become a Great Tree like me!"

Following that conversation, Zerah had no longer been afraid of the great distance between his branch and the ground.

Then one day, Zerah had seen another Great Tree, almost as great as his own, harmed by the Wind. There had been a storm one night. Loud claps of thunder had banished the stillness. Lightning had cracked open the sky. The Wind had howled like an animal in pain. The sunrise that morning had revealed what the night had concealed: that the Wind had uprooted the Almost-As-Great Great Tree.

The fear that had taken hold of Zerah's heart on seeing the Wind's destruction might never have released its grip had it not been for a friendly spider. Resting in her web just above his head, she had imparted a truth that his Great Tree had not yet told him. There were two Winds: the Good Wind and the Bad Wind.

"The Bad Wind does bad things," the Spider had explained. "It sometimes even does cruel things—that means *very* bad."

She had said that the Bad Wind yanked roots skywards and plunged branches into the earth; that it shredded birds' nests, tore spiderwebs apart, laid waste to fruit, and withered flowers before their time; that it destroyed beauty and exchanged life for death; that it turned dreams into nightmares. The Bad Wind never felt remorse for what it did. It was something the Spider called *indifferent*. It didn't care about anyone or anything.

Then there was the Good Wind. The Good Wind rocked Zerah to sleep every night, humming lullabies as it did so. The Good Wind woke him each morning with tender kisses and sweet whispers, which sounded to Zerah like promises of great things to come. The Good Wind made still branches shake with laughter, causing them to swing him back and forth through the sky. The Good Wind enabled silent leaves to join the chorus of birds and cicadas, and when they did, Zerah learned that song was not only something he could hear, but also something he would one day make. The Good Wind carried the scent of ripening fruit to his nose like a never-ending gift that said, "Take," and then, "Take more." The Good Wind encircled him with an aroma of flowers so close and so strong that, for a moment, Zerah thought he was the source of that sweetness. The Good Wind doubled beauty. The Good Wind ensured eternal life. The Good Wind wanted Zerah to root himself and find love. The Good Wind cared.

"But how can I be sure that the Good Wind will protect me from the Bad Wind?" Zerah had asked the Spider.

The Spider had gestured to her web.

"Do you see how small and wispy my web is compared with a Great Tree?" she had asked him.

Zerah had nodded.

"It withstood the storm. How is that possible, when the Great Tree beside us was uprooted?"

Zerah had eyed the remains of the Almost-As-Great Great Tree and then looked at the spiderweb again, feeling baffled. "I don't know."

The Spider had spoken with as much certainty as Zerah's Great Tree always had.

"Because the Good Wind protects the good from the Bad Wind. The Good Wind will protect you, because you are good."

Zerah hadn't questioned the Spider's words, nor what they implied about the Uprooted Tree. He had only compared the Spider's words with his own experiences. He had never been harmed by the Wind.

But right now, Zerah was thinking of the Uprooted Tree. She hadn't been bad, and neither had her branches, leaves, fruit, flowers, and seeds; nor those who had made their home in her.

Zerah thought of his journey from the moment he had left his Great Tree until the time he had arrived in the desert. He had never once ceased to feel the Wind around him. Its touch had been gentle, then firm, then tight, but it had never ceased to be. It had never let go of him so that the Bad Wind could take hold of him. The Wind that had carried him to the brownish-red patch of earth was the same one that had taken him from it and left him in the desert. There could only be one Wind.

Is the Wind compassionate at times and cruel at others? Or completely and utterly indifferent? Zerah questioned. Neither possibility filled his heart with peace. It didn't matter to him that the Wind had returned to the desert. He felt the Wind had already shown its lack of concern by bringing him there; that it had already betrayed him. *How can I ever trust the Wind again?*

Zerah had once believed that the only thing that could take root was a seed in the ground. Now he knew that this was not so. Truths could also take root, and the uprooting of those truths was painful.

Why did the Spider lie to me? Did she want to cause me pain, like the Wind? Was she bad? Or was she just indifferent?

Zerah mourned for the Wind and what it had done to his present, his future, and his past. His new understanding of the Wind had affected what lay behind him as much as before him. As Zerah thought back to his nights growing on the Great Tree, when the Wind had cradled and sung to him, and to the mornings when he had been awakened by the same gentle rocking that had lulled him to sleep, he found that every one of those memories had been wrung empty of its sweetness.

Zerah had no idea how long he had remained buried in the sand, mourning for the Wind. Hidden from the sky, the days and nights merged into one long stretch of sameness. Time became something that mattered again—something that could be filled with the differences that distinguished one moment from another—after Zerah heard the words, "Are you OK?" Had those words not been spoken, or had Zerah not heard them, he might still be buried in the sand today.

Zerah raised his head slightly above the sand and looked around.

"Grain of Sand?" he said.

There were countless grains of sand, but he saw no sign of the First Grain of Sand he had met, nor the Second.

"No," said the voice. "I'm not a grain of sand."

"Who are you?"

"Look up."

Zerah gazed upwards. He saw something green. *Can it be?* he wondered. He gazed higher and saw more green. *Is it really so?* He looked higher still and saw even more green. *Yes, it is. A tree!*

Zerah couldn't believe it. *The First Grain of Sand was right. There are trees in the desert!*

He wasn't a Great Tree, that was for sure. He was a little tree. A pointy tree. An ugly tree! Truth be told, he looked so unlike any tree Zerah had seen before that he wasn't completely sure this really was a tree. But he was green. He had two branches, of a sort. And atop him grew a single flower and a single piece of fruit.

And then he spoke. "I am a little tree."

Zerah grinned at the Little Tree. "I am Zerah."

Then his smile faded. "And I am a lost, abandoned little seed."

"Dear Zerah," said the Little Tree soothingly. "How can you be lost when wherever you are is where you're meant to be? And how can you think you're abandoned when you're never alone?"

Zerah surveyed the strange Little Tree. Even though he had been buried in the sand for quite some time, and even though the Little Tree really was a *little* tree, surely, he could not have rooted himself and grown so quickly while Zerah had been beneath the sand.

Zerah realized he must have been moved from one part of the desert to another without even noticing. *Yet how can that be?* he questioned. *Does the shifting of the sands at the top affect the shifting of the sands at the bottom? Is the Wind that powerful?*

Thinking back to the tree that had been uprooted, Zerah knew that the Wind was indeed that strong. It seemed there was no escaping the Wind! *Was it the Wind that buried me beneath the grains of sand? If it was, why didn't it bury me beneath specks of soil instead?*

"I hate you, Wind," Zerah mumbled under his breath.

"Did you say 'Wind'?" asked the Little Tree. His eyes opened wide like a flower greeting the dawn.

Before Zerah could respond, the Little Tree cleared his throat, hummed a couple of notes, took a deep breath, and then began to sing as loudly as he could:

> *Oh, beautiful Wind! Oh, gracious Wind!*
> *You are indivisible!*
> *Oh, loving Wind! Oh, tender Wind!*
> *You make joyous the miserable!*
> *You are always good!*
> *You are always kind!*
> *I praise you in*
> *My heart and mind!*

What's this? thought Zerah.

The Little Tree took another deep breath and sang on:

> *Oh, correct Wind! Oh, caring Wind!*
> *You are everywhere I see!*
> *Oh, powerful Wind! Oh, happy Wind!*
> *Your love always surrounds me!*

Zerah interrupted the Little Tree. He was certain that if he heard one more verse of *Oh Wind*, he would be ill. "Little Tree, I don't know you, but I know the Wind. Its heart is indifferent, and its actions are cruel. Why are you singing praises to it?"

The Little Tree gasped. "Indifferent? Never! Cruel? Never ever! How can you say such a thing? Oh, Wind, forgive him! He knows not what he says!"

Zerah groaned. "Oh yes I do! And I can say such things because of what I've seen. Bad things!"

Zerah looked at the Little Tree with disgust. At that moment, he could think of nothing worse than the Wind, except for a loud, out-of-tune little tree singing praises to it.

"Bad things done by the Wind?" the Little Tree asked, stunned. "That's just not possible!"

Zerah rolled his eyes. "Oh yeah?" he challenged. "How about uprooting a tree?"

The Little Tree spoke serenely. "Maybe the tree it uprooted was sick and dying. Or perhaps he was about to be cut down, and the Wind wanted to spare him a greater pain. Maybe the Wind needed to clear a space for a seed to root herself. I don't know what the Wind's reasons were. I just know that it always has reasons, and that they are always good."

"Ha! And how do you know that? Did the Wind tell you so?"

The Little Tree blushed. "The Wind talk to me? The Great Wind talk to a little tree like me? You must be joking! Why, the very thought of it! Oh! Oh! Oh!" He began to shake.

"OK, OK!" Zerah shouted. "Calm down!"

The Little Tree composed himself.

"All I meant was that if the Wind doesn't tell you what its reasons are, how can you be sure that they are good?"

"It's called faith," replied the Little Tree.

"What is that?" asked Zerah.

"Faith is what a seed has when he believes that he will become a tree."

"But I don't just *believe* I will become a tree—a *Great* Tree—I *know* it!" Zerah exclaimed with certainty. However, a single thought in his head set his heart trembling with doubt: *I just don't yet know how or where…*

The Little Tree spoke again. "Just as *I know* that the Wind is good." He smiled curiously. "Tell me, Zerah, did the Wind tell *you* its reasons for uprooting the tree?"

"No," Zerah said.

"Well then, how can *you* be so sure that its reasons were *not* good?"

Zerah thought about this for a moment. Maybe he couldn't be sure. Then his memories of the Uprooted Tree returned to the past, and his present reality took its place. Words fell heavy and hard from Zerah's lips, like a downpour from the clouds.

"If the Wind is always so good and correct, why did it bring me here to the desert? It was supposed to carry me to a field!"

"Oh, Zerah," the Little Tree said consolingly. "Once I thought like you. Once

I thought, *I will become a tree growing by the side of an oasis.* Then when I was blown here instead of there, I got very angry with the Wind and with the world. Yet why, of all the places I could grow, did I think I would end up by the side of an oasis? Because that's what I had been told. But it wasn't the Wind who told me that. Think back, Zerah. Did the Wind ever tell you it would carry you to a field?"

Zerah cast his mind back. He remembered being told, "When it is time for you to drop, the Wind will carry you in its embrace to a field where you will root yourself and become a Great Tree."

The Wind had not spoken these words; his Great Tree had.

Zerah cried out to the Little Tree. "It was my Great Tree who told me so! He lied! Why would he tell me the Wind would take me to a field if he didn't know where the Wind would take me?"

"I don't think your Great Tree lied," said the Little Tree. "I think he told you what he believed."

"But what he believed was wrong! How could my Great Tree not know the difference between beliefs and truths?"

"Many do not know the difference between beliefs and truths. In fact, to some there is no difference at all."

Zerah was silent for a moment as he contemplated the Little Tree's words.

Maybe the Spider's lie about the Wind wasn't a lie at all; only a belief she considered to be a truth. Maybe my Great Tree's certainty about what the Wind would do came from his own experience of the Wind. Perhaps when my Great Tree was a seed, the Wind carried him directly from the branch on which he had grown to the ground in which he had rooted himself.

Yet my Great Tree knew at least one other whose plans had been changed by the Wind: the Uprooted Tree. So hadn't he known that it was possible for my plans to be changed as well? Maybe he believed the Good Wind would root me in a field, and that the Bad Wind had uprooted the Almost-As-Great Great Tree?

But as I grew, I understood that there were not two Winds, but one. Did my Great Tree, like the Spider, never outgrow that belief?

Zerah thought back to the words the First Grain of Sand had spoken, and finally understood how one could grow even without developing roots. *But how could it be that my Great Tree didn't know the things that I, only a seed, now know? Are there other things my Great Tree didn't know?*

Zerah eyed the Little Tree. The scent of his fruit was a sweet companion to the soft breeze. His flower was swaying, carefree. His eyes were closed. He was rocking back and forth, chanting, "Wind, Wind, Wind." He was in ecstasy.

Meanwhile, Zerah was in agony. *What can I believe in now that my beliefs are gone? If I can't be certain that the Wind will take me to a field, what can I be certain of?* He asked the Little Tree these questions.

The Little Tree smiled reassuringly. "You can believe in the Wind. You can be certain that there is one Wind, and that it loves you. You can be certain that the Wind will help you root yourself where you are most needed. You know what you want, but the Wind knows what you and every other being in the world needs. Trust the Wind, Zerah. It is wiser than both of us."

With that, the Little Tree began to sing his song of praise again:

Oh great Wind! Oh special Wind!

Zerah rolled over in the desert breeze, turning away from the Little Tree and his song. But he could still hear the Little Tree's words in his head and heart; a strange echo that strengthened rather than diminished. He began to think about those words: "You can be certain that the Wind will help you root yourself where you are most needed."

Zerah considered his time in the desert and all that he had suffered there. *Is it the desert itself that has caused me so much pain and sorrow, or my belief about what should be happening in my life?* he wondered.

Thoughts of the Uprooted Tree again filled his mind. *Was it possible that she had been sick and dying, and I just never realized it? Or that she had been about to be cut down? Perhaps her uprooting is proof of the Wind's compassion, rather than its cruelty.*

Maybe her uprooting was necessary in order to create a place for a seed to take root.

Zerah surveyed the desert around him. *What if the Wind brought me here on purpose? Perhaps it wants me to learn something essential to help me become a Great Tree. I've already learned that there's a difference between beliefs and truths. I will spare my own seeds all this suffering by simply telling them, "You can be certain that the Wind will help you root yourself where you are most needed, and you will become a Great Tree there."*

Perhaps, Zerah reflected, *I am most needed here in the desert.*

He thought back to the nighttime tales of forests his Great Tree had told all the seeds. *Maybe the Wind brought me to the desert to transform it into a forest! How loved would I be then?! I suppose I don't truly know why the Wind brought me here, but I have faith that the Wind knows. And when it's ready, it will share that knowledge with me.* Zerah smiled at how wise he had already become. *Perhaps I will not become a Great Tree, but a Greater Tree!* Zerah's smile grew very wide indeed.

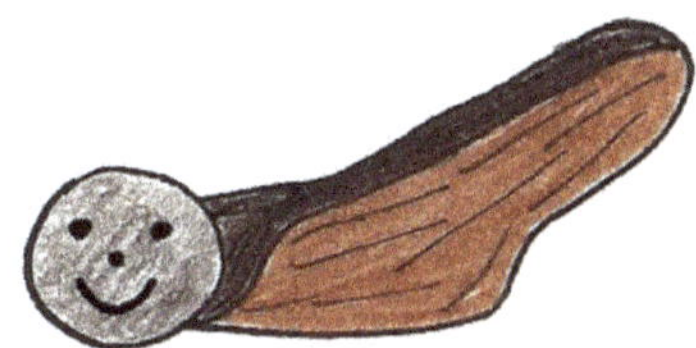

From that moment on, Zerah felt different. A large part of the empty space in his heart was now filled: filled with the Wind. *I must be important, and useful, and special! If I wasn't, the Wind wouldn't have gone to so much trouble to teach me!*

Zerah's memories of the Wind grew sweet again. The past became a joyous place to visit once more. The tremendous love he felt in the present forged a path towards the love waiting in his future. And the desert became an enchanting place, filled with great wisdom and as much beauty as a sky full of stars.

Did the desert change or did I? Zerah wondered. It didn't seem possible that the desert in which he was living and learning, by the grace of the Wind, was the same one in which he had felt stuck, lost, abandoned, and grief-stricken such a short time ago due to the Wind's apparent cruelty and indifference.

In this new desert, the sun set leaving the faithless in darkness and the faithful in the eternal light of the sun within them. The moon glowed full and round, speaking of wholeness and telling old tales about that which can change: one's own self. The music of the owls, crickets, and bees filled up Zerah's ears, and the Wind's moans became notes in a serenade. Dust particles and grains of sand whirled in the air beside Zerah. He joined in with their movements, becoming the dance of the near and soon. Every moment was the same as the one that had come before it; each a moment in which he was loved by the Wind.

"Why did you bring me here, Wind?" Zerah had once asked over and over again. Now, every moment he lived was an exquisite answer to that question: to become a Greater Tree.

Perhaps, if I learn everything the Wind wants me to, I will become the Greatest Tree that ever was! Then the whole world will not only know me, but need me! The whole world will love me!

Zerah felt like the most important, useful, and special seed there was. He was the happiest he could ever remember being.

The seed of truth the Little Tree had planted was taking root in Zerah's heart, where the old "truth" had once lived. With each passing day, the roots grew deeper and the new truth felt stronger, rising up like a tree inside him. Its branches stretched far beyond its roots; up into his head, where they yielded new thoughts.

With a love like the Wind's, how had the Spider's beliefs ever come to be? Are there other truths that are only beliefs? What are they? And what are all these lessons the Wind wants me to learn?

Hungry to grow and learn, Zerah found many who were willing to teach.

From a raindrop, he learned that, though the dew gave little and a downpour much, sometimes the dew was sweeter because it shared all from the little it had.

How important! thought Zerah. He pledged to consume dew and downpour in equal measure. His future fruit and flowers became so sweet in his mind that he could already taste and smell them.

From the ground, Zerah learned that stretching his roots out far and deep so they would know many new grains of sand, rather than clinging to a few familiar ones, would help him grow bigger and stronger.

How useful! he thought. His imagined trunk doubled in size, his branches reached three times as far, and every single leaf unfurled at once. The tremendous open space beneath his canopy offered shade to so many diverse creatures that Zerah saw rainbows below him as well as in the sky. He couldn't wait to root himself as soon as the Wind became still enough for him to do so. Or as soon as it carried him to a place beyond the desert, providing that was the Wind's will.

From three humans, two of whom praised a butterfly's blue and black wings, while the third criticized them for not being orange and gold, Zerah learned nothing. But the One Hundred and Eighteenth Grain of Sand Zerah met told him otherwise.

"Everyone and everything in this world teaches us something," the Grain of Sand told Zerah. "Perhaps it is what to do; perhaps it is what not to do. Just make sure you know the difference."

Ah, thought Zerah. *I will learn from the butterfly's mistake. I will make sure my flowers are not just the colors of the sunrise, but of the sky and grass, and even the grains of sand. Then I will be perfect, and not only will I be happy, but I will make everyone else happy.*

On and on the Wind blew Zerah, and Zerah learned more and more.

Zerah learned that beauty was a feeling in one's heart, and not a vision before one's eyes. *It is love that makes the desert beautiful,* he marveled. When the Wind blew him past the Little Tree, Zerah couldn't believe his eyes. Love had transformed even the ugly Little Tree into an exquisite one.

Zerah discovered that there were not two names for the Wind—Wind and Breeze—but many: Gust, Gale, Zephyr, and Current of Air. He learned that, though there were many names for the Wind, there was still only one Wind. There was one Wind, but it was everywhere: caressing the grains of sand to his left and right; before him, behind him, and below him; as well as swirling in the sky above him; blowing in the distance beyond him; and dancing inside his heart.

A praying mantis taught Zerah that while not all beings had the Wind inside their hearts, the Wind had everyone and everything in existence inside its heart, "for such is the great love of the Great Wind."

Zerah learned of other beliefs masquerading as truths, and he found them utterly heartbreaking.

There was the Teeny Beetle who believed the Wind wanted everyone to suffer. "We are bad. Therefore, we must be punished! Bad things must happen to us!"

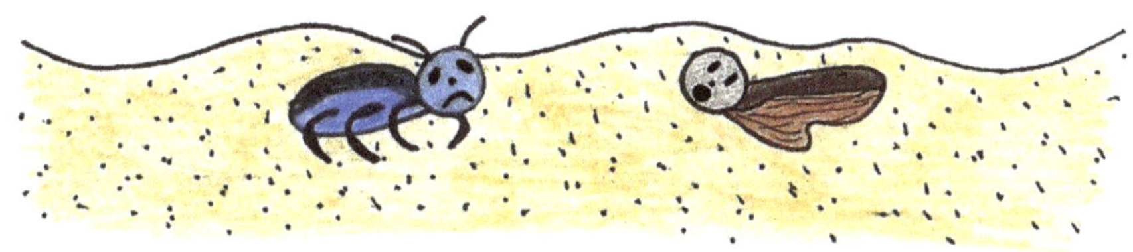

"Why are we bad?" Zerah asked.

The Teeny Beetle pointed to the world around her and then to herself. "Because everything is wrong! Spiders refuse to stop weaving their webs and birds refuse to stop singing. Not all butterflies are attracted to the same flowers' scents. Bees want to decide what to do with their own wings. They reject the counsel of a tiny mouse I know. He has offered to teach them where and how to fly. Armadillos have tails. Geckos, mosquitoes, and crickets don't look like fleas. And I have six legs instead of eight!"

"Huh?" was all Zerah could manage in response. *If the Teeny Beetle believes such nonsense, how can I disprove it with sense? After all, if butterflies are all supposed to like the same scent, why do different scents exist? If everyone and everything looked exactly the same, what would exist? If spiders are so bad, why does the Teeny Beetle want eight legs like them? If the Tiny Mouse was meant to decide what to do with wings, wouldn't he have his own?*

Then there was the Large Spine from a cactus who believed the Wind wanted him to scatter as many grains of sand as possible.

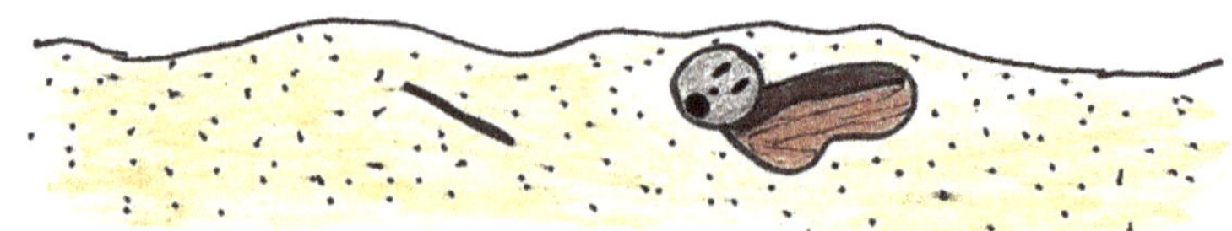

"Ah, how I dream of scattering! Of sending grains of sand far from their homes, and then slicing them in two if they try to return! The Wind gave the desert to me, not to them! Oh, if only I had legs or wings," the Large Spine bemoaned.

Thank the Wind you don't! Zerah thought. *If the Wind wanted grains of sand to be scattered and sliced in two, the Wind would indeed be bad. Who would ever do what such a Wind said? Why does the Large Spine not understand that just as the sky has enough space for all who fly within it, so too does the desert have enough space for all who dwell there? Why does he want to force grains of sand from their homes?*

As the Wind carried Zerah away, he felt grateful that the Wind loved everyone enough to protect them from the Teeny Beetle, Tiny Mouse, and Large Spine, and to make it impossible for them to turn their beliefs into actions. Zerah wondered again, *With a love like the Wind's, how could such beliefs ever come to be? How could such incomprehensible things ever be believed?* But no matter how much he pondered that question, he still couldn't find an answer. *Well, lessons are more important than questions and answers,* he decided.

Then his lessons continued.

Zerah learned that, despite their similar appearances, no two grains of sand were alike. Like every seed, each grain of sand was unique.

He also discovered that, though the grains of sand could not offer him shade or food, they could and did offer him many other things.

"Everyone and everything offers something," said the Two Hundred and Thirty-Sixth Grain of Sand Zerah met. "An offering can be an action. It can be words. It can be something that is held in a hand or a paw. It can also be something that is held in the heart or the head."

"Like teachings?" Zerah asked.

"Yes, like teachings," the Grain of Sand replied. "We offer what we have to give; that is, what we have been given and have accepted, for not all offerings need be accepted. We can accept and we can reject."

"How?"

"It is called power," explained the Grain the Sand.

"Power is what the Wind has," Zerah said.

"Power is what we all have," stated the Grain of Sand. "We can accept or reject things because we have the power to do so. But remember: we are not always conscious of what we accept and what we reject, just as we are not always conscious of what we give and what we withhold."

Zerah considered everything he had been offered in his life up to that moment. He thought of what he had accepted, such as the truth about the Wind, and what he had rejected, such as the beliefs of the Spider, the Second Grain of Sand, the Teeny Beetle, and the Large Spine.

I do have power, thought Zerah. *And I have already used it.*

Zerah tried to think of what he had accepted, rejected, given, and withheld unconsciously, but of course, he could not. Without being conscious of these things, it was impossible to think about them.

Then Zerah wondered what he had offered. He hadn't provided houses or a place to rest. He hadn't given fruit. He hadn't created anything beautiful. He had done nothing of any significance. *What can a little seed give, after all?* he asked himself.

But when he thought of the friendship he had offered Semeeya, joy and contentment swelled so much within his heart that he felt their reach beyond it, raising the corners of his mouth and crinkling his eyes. His body felt light, as it did when the Wind lifted him off the ground.

When Zerah looked within his heart to see more, he also found the cruel words he had offered the First Grain of Sand. Sorrow and regret stirred within him, and they, too, had the power to give birth to actions. His smile sank and his eyes clouded over. He felt too heavy for the Wind to carry. Before Zerah could see any more, he looked away from his heart and back to the desert.

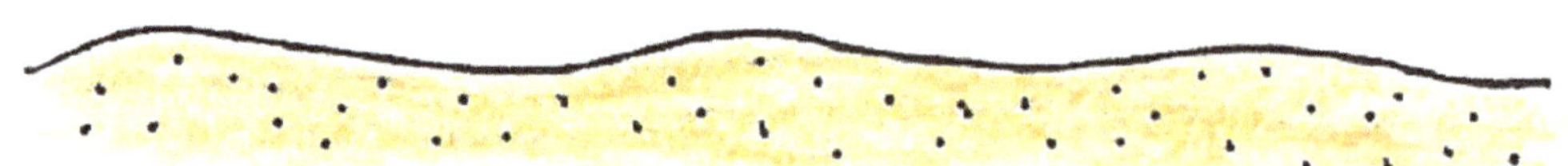

His lessons continued.

From a cloud and a snake, Zerah learned that others aside from seeds and grains of sand had dreams, though often their dreams were quite different from his own.

"I dream of a life spent wandering the earth," said the Cloud.

"I dream of a life spent floating in the sky," said the Snake.

From a human who was talking to himself, Zerah learned that some creatures dreamed dreams quite similar to his own: "I dream of transforming the desert into a city."

Zerah didn't know what a city was, but he knew that transformation meant change. *His dream of changing the desert into a city is like my dream of turning it into a forest: it is the dream of doing something great and becoming someone great because of it.*

And from the Desert itself, Zerah learned that sometimes changed plans were the greatest teaching and blessing of all.

If the Wind had a plan for Zerah, it was not that he would root himself in the desert. One day, along came a tiny breeze that picked Zerah up. Then the breeze became a strong gust, and the strong gust became an even stronger gale. Before Zerah knew what was happening, he was high above the desert, swirling in the sky.

Zerah was calm. After all, as long as he always traveled with the Wind, what did it matter where he traveled to? He winked at the clouds as he soared through the sky on the wings of the Wind, and the enormous grin he offered the grains of sand spinning beside him not only caused them to smile, but also allayed the fears of the tiniest grains, who had been raised off the ground for the first time in their lives.

When Zerah finally looked down, he saw clumps of soil and blades of grass instead of grains of sand. His world of tan was green once more. Zerah was out of the desert. He had not grown roots there, though he had surely grown. Zerah was not the same seed he had been on arrival many sunsets and sunrises before.

Despite Zerah's supreme faith in the Wind, he couldn't help but feel disappointed as the fields below him soon became the fields behind him. Buildings much bigger than the single house next to the field in which he had grown came into view. They were tall; taller even than his Great Tree! They were slick and silver, and stood so close together that each one's reflection was multiplied many times over. It was a world of sameness, in which each building saw nothing but itself.

The Wind set Zerah down gently on a very hard surface.

Zerah looked around. There was no soil, blades of grass, trees or insects. He looked a little closer. He saw animals, but only a few: a couple of birds off in the distance and a dog running in zigzags with something clenched between her teeth. He did, however, see plenty of humans. Some of them walked quickly across the ground on which he lay; so quickly, in fact, that they almost stepped on him! They surely would

have done so had a breeze not shifted him slightly to the left or right just in time.

"Watch it!" Zerah cried out as a human's foot almost came down hard on his head. But the human was too distracted to hear him.

The humans are certainly in a hurry to do something, thought Zerah. *But what could be more important than making sure they don't step on a seed?*

As more humans rushed by, Zerah's annoyance turned into concern. *Oh dear! They definitely need a place to rest!* Then he noticed that some humans didn't rush at all. Instead, they lay like Zerah on the hard surface covering the ground. *Oh no! They need homes as much as the ants and birds!* Zerah saw other humans eating rotting fruit. "Oh no, no!" he cried out in a loud voice. "They desperately need food!"

Zerah didn't understand. He wondered how—in a world where trees refused not one insect, animal or human that reached for their fruit or leaned in close to know the secrets of their flowers' scents; where trees even let their fruit fall and sent their flowers' perfume off to travel with the Wind, halving the work of a harvest and making a journey to sweetness unnecessary—there could exist a place like this, filled with rotting fruit, hunger so unbearable that one consumed such decay, and air that hurt to breathe. How could it be? And why?

Even though Zerah understood that beauty was a choice one made with one's heart rather than a vision before one's eyes, and that if love could make an ugly tree and a desert beautiful, it could most surely make the hard, gray ground and silver buildings beautiful, he felt certain that a flower or two growing on a tree in this strange and troublesome place would make that choice far easier.

Zerah still longed for a field. When he closed his eyes, he could see it: green blades of grass crowned in gold; each dewdrop cradling the light of the sun. When he sent his imagination further and further from his current life, he could actually feel them: moist specks of soil offering him the embrace that would make countless other embraces possible. He could smell the rain and hear the drops seeping into the earth one by one. He swallowed the nourishment they gave him, and his first root grew. Then there was nothing left to do but wait for his dream to be fulfilled.

Zerah opened his eyes. It was all gone.

He tried to console himself. *As the Little Tree taught me, who am I to question the wisdom of the Wind? He told me: "The Wind will help you root yourself where you are most needed." I am certainly needed here! But where, exactly, is here?*

"Where am I?" Zerah asked aloud.

"You are in a city," said a voice.

"And what is that?" asked Zerah.

"That is this!" replied the same voice.

"And where are you?" Zerah questioned, turning his head from side to side.

"Look down."

Zerah looked at the hard surface below him, puzzled. "Who are you?"

"I am a sidewalk," said the Sidewalk.

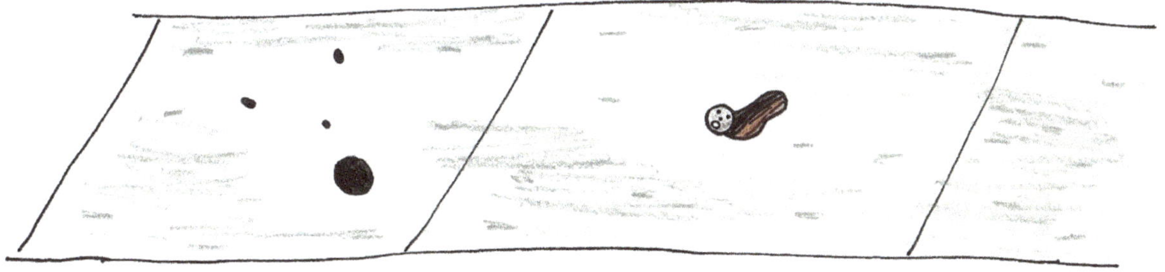

Zerah waited for the Sidewalk to ask him who he was, but the Sidewalk didn't ask. Instead, he continued speaking about himself.

"But not just *any* sidewalk. I am the Greatest Sidewalk that ever was, and that will ever be! I have the smoothest, flattest surface. I have no holes or cracks. I have shards of minerals inside me, and they dazzle in the light of the golden streetlamps and in the reflection of the silver buildings. I transform the uneven ground into a level surface so the humans can move quickly in the correct direction, and in an orderly way. I stop blades of grass from growing; I smother them. I prevent seeds from becoming trees; I don't even let them take root. And oh, how I am admired for my cunning, extolled for my incredible feats, and worshipped for my power! Oh, how I am loved!"

The Sidewalk beamed as though a crowd surrounded him, serenading him with praise. Zerah listened for the praise, but all he heard was the tap-tap-tapping of human feet, stepping down quickly, lifting even faster, then stepping again. The speedy humans didn't even seem to be aware of the Sidewalk. *How can you possibly love and care about someone or something if you don't even know they exist?* Zerah wondered, as another foot nearly stepped upon his back. *They pay no attention to what is below them.*

As for the Sidewalk, he doesn't seem to be aware that, even though he has power, everyone else does as well. And as for the rest of the Sidewalk's claims, they sound like lies. Who wouldn't want a tree? Who would want to stop blades of grass from growing? Who would love anyone or anything that hurt either one of them?

"Excuse me," Zerah said to the Sidewalk.

The Sidewalk was busy giving directions to the humans. "You, to the left; you, to the right. That's it, that's it. Move along! No, don't turn there. Turn here. Faster now. *Faster!*"

"Sidewalk!" Zerah yelled.

The Sidewalk kept his eyes on the humans. After he had made sure their steps were straight, their pace swift, and their movements under control, he shifted his gaze towards the sound of the tiny voice. His eyes widened and his mouth hung open as he took Zerah in.

"You're still here?"

Zerah looked at the Sidewalk, dumbfounded. "Of course I'm still here! The air is still. Where else would I be?"

Only half paying attention, the Sidewalk smiled knowingly. "You'll find out soon enough."

"I want to find out now!" Zerah demanded. "I want to know why you said that you stop blades of grass from growing and prevent seeds from becoming trees."

The Sidewalk smirked. "I prefer the word *smother*. I smother blades of grass because they are blades of grass. And I prevent seeds from taking root because I have to," said the Sidewalk matter-of-factly.

Zerah was no less bewildered. "I don't think you understand," Zerah explained, his words slow and clear. "Blades of grass are *supposed to* grow. And seeds are *supposed to* become Great Trees. And I, well, I was born to become the Greatest Tree."

"No, *you* don't understand," the Sidewalk snarled. "You see, I was born to stop seeds from becoming any kind of tree at all. And I'm doing quite a good job of it, thank you very much. I mean, look around you. Do you see a single tree? Or, for that matter, a single flower? A single patch of grass?"

It was true. Zerah could not see a single tree, flower, or blade of grass. But having lived so long in the desert, Zerah knew that first impressions weren't always accurate. Somewhere close by he was sure there was at least a little tree, a tiny flower, and a single blade of grass.

Having learned so much in the desert, Zerah also understood that he didn't have to accept the fear and lies the Sidewalk was offering him. He remembered that he had the power to accept and the power to reject. He also had the power to make an offering of his own. What kind of offering would it be? One of anger? Hatred?

The Sidewalk is probably only repeating what he has been taught, Zerah reasoned. *Perhaps he was never taught about seeds, just as I was never taught about the Wind; taught correctly, that is. Poor, poor Sidewalk. I will teach him.*

Zerah turned toward the Sidewalk, ready to explain seeds and trees to him; ready to explain life. He began very gently.

"The Wind—"

Before Zerah could say another word, the Sidewalk cut him off.

"The Wind? What is that?"

"What do you mean, what is that?" asked Zerah, stunned. "The Wind is the Wind."

There was a blank look on the Sidewalk's face.

Zerah recited all the other names he knew for the Wind. Still, the Sidewalk was uncomprehending.

Zerah searched for an explanation. "The thing that makes other things move from one place to another."

"Legs?" asked the Sidewalk. "Wings?"

"No! The thing that brought me here! The *Wind!*"

The Sidewalk groaned. "The thing that brought you here was a fall from the sky. The thing that will take you from here is a bird eating you, or a human crushing you, or a broom sweeping you up with the garbage!"

Zerah stared at the Sidewalk. He didn't know what *crushing* meant. Nor did he know what a *broom, sweeping,* or *garbage* were. But he knew that birds ate worms, not seeds. And he knew that the Wind had brought him there, whether the Sidewalk knew what it was or not.

In the desert, Zerah had met many who believed, as he once had, that the Wind was cruel or indifferent. But not once had he met anyone who didn't know what the Wind was; who entirely denied its existence!

Grains of Sand who don't know what trees are. Sidewalks who don't know what the Wind is. How is that possible? wondered Zerah, amazed at their ignorance. Then he heard his heart ask: "What is there in life that I don't know?"

He heard Life's reply: "A great deal."

But not knowing felt scary, like a life without the Wind, or a seed without a friend, or a city without a tree. So Zerah hushed his heart and turned back toward the Sidewalk. He decided to concentrate on what he knew; on answers instead of questions. He would show the Sidewalk what the Wind was.

Zerah looked around for proof of the Wind's existence: a tree's leaves swaying, a flower's petals fluttering, blades of grass bending. Then he remembered there were no trees, flowers, or blades of grass in sight.

"Move along!" the Sidewalk commanded as another human scurried past.

Zerah watched as the human's hair danced, lifted from his shoulders and twirled by an invisible partner.

"There!" Zerah shouted. "Right there! Do you see that human's hair moving? It is the Wind that's moving it!"

The Sidewalk rolled his eyes. "It is Speed that's moving it. I wonder what will come along to move you!"

Zerah was exasperated. A slight breeze came along and shifted him a little to the left, safely away from another human's foot.

"Did you feel *that*?" Zerah demanded.

"Feel what? I didn't feel anything. Now, if you don't mind, I have blades of grass to smother and directions to give. So, no more questions and no more bothering me!"

The Sidewalk resumed his barking orders, but spoke not another word to Zerah.

Zerah sighed. *Oh well, I tried. And I guess I've learned another lesson: you can't teach someone who doesn't want to learn. Unless…* A tiny smirk raised the corners of Zerah's mouth. *Perhaps one day the Wind will come along and uproot this Sidewalk! Then he'll know what the Wind is!* Zerah imagined the Sidewalk overturned, and in his place a forest; perhaps even a forest full of his own future trees.

Then Zerah did the only thing he knew how to do: he sat and waited for the Wind to take him someplace. He wondered if it would take him into one of the buildings so he could learn his next lesson. Or to a patch of earth, that most surely existed somewhere in the city, so that he could root himself where he was truly needed. Or, as he still hoped, in the very depths of his heart, to a field.

But the Wind did not take Zerah anywhere. In fact, it seemed to have vanished. For six sunsets and sunrises, no human's hair danced. Not a single feather was ruffled when the birds were not in flight. Zerah's body was still, and in almost the exact same place as when he had first arrived in the city. No human stepped upon him; however, the Wind failed to offer even the slightest breeze as a reassurance that it would move Zerah out of the way if necessary. Like the Sidewalk, Zerah did not feel the Wind. But unlike the Sidewalk, Zerah constantly told himself: *Just because I cannot feel the Wind's presence with my body, see it with my eyes, or hear it with my ears, that doesn't mean it doesn't exist, or that it isn't here with me right now. I can feel it in my heart. I can see it dancing there. I can hear it singing still.*

Zerah attempted to speak with the speedy humans while he waited for the Wind to return. But unlike the grains of sand in the desert, the speedy humans in the city didn't answer when Zerah spoke to them. They didn't even notice him.

I suppose, Zerah eventually decided, *that I am learning yet again what not to do. When I become the Greatest Tree, I shall notice those who are less than me, like the speedy humans, and speak with them.*

Zerah was just about to turn towards a human eating rotting fruit when the Wind came along.

"I knew it!" Zerah rejoiced. "Once I learned what you brought me here to teach me, I knew you would take me to the place I need to be next! I knew you hadn't left me! I know how much you love me!"

The Wind dropped Zerah just a little further to the right of where he had been lying. It did so just in time for Zerah to see another speedy human hurrying across the Sidewalk; just in time for Zerah to realize that he was in the human's path; just in time for Zerah to understand that "crushed" was the same thing as being stepped on, and that it was about to happen to him if the Wind didn't come along and move him once again! Then, in the space of a breath, the human's foot came down hard on Zerah's back, and he was crushed.

"Ooow!" Zerah howled in pain.

Unaware that a seed's life had just been changed forever, the human hurried along on her way.

The Sidewalk sneered. "I told you, didn't I? I warned you, didn't I?"

Zerah could not respond. He could barely even breathe. His body was split down the middle. A large piece of it was severed, and there were fractures to one side of his head and what remained of his body. Wincing, Zerah turned his head to see just how much of him was broken. It felt like his entire self. The sight of his crushed body pierced like a rose's thorn into his heart. Pain oozed everywhere. Robbed of all reason, his mind could think of only one question.

"Why?" Zerah asked, his voice slight, his breathing strained. "Taking me to a desert to teach me how to better live my life? *That*, I understand. But bringing me to a city so that my life might end? Why, Wind? *Why?*"

The Wind did not answer.

Zerah remained on the Sidewalk, weeping and shattered, until a dog ran past him so quickly that her speed created a breeze, which in turn caused Zerah to be blown to an isolated part of the Sidewalk, and then into a very tiny, very deep, very dark hole. Inside that abyss, Zerah's pain carved two more questions into his heart. His despair immediately answered them.

How can I ever root myself now?

You cannot.

Who could ever love me now?

No one.

Up until the point when he had been crushed, Zerah had been waiting hopefully for the Wind. Now, his body broken, his beliefs destroyed, his heart empty of hope, Zerah waited for death.

THE SUN SET many times over. Still, Zerah waited. The moon waned. Still, Zerah waited. Nothing and no one sang. The dance of the here and now, and of the near and soon, resigned themselves to the eternal sleep of never. Each moment that came found Zerah doing exactly what he had done in the previous moment: waiting for death to come. Then one day he realized that death had *already* come. It was not the death his Great Tree had taught him about, but it was a death nonetheless.

While growing on his Great Tree, Zerah had seen death. Before he had fallen from his branch, many of his Great Tree's leaves had done so. He had watched them from high above as they lay motionless on the ground. But soon after they fell, transformation began. The colors in their bodies faded. They turned brittle and frail. They crumbled bit by bit until they no longer resembled leaves but became part of the earth itself. Zerah had also seen the Uprooted Tree. Though the Uprooted Tree had been carried away by humans, her fallen leaves, rotting fruit, and withered flowers had been left behind. They had been transformed, just like his Great Tree's leaves.

"What is this?" Zerah had asked his Great Tree. "When a thing changes its colors and form and becomes something else, what is it called?"

"It is called death," his Great Tree had told him. "And it will happen to us all at some point."

"Even to *you*?" Zerah had asked, wide-eyed.

"Even to me," his Great Tree had answered.

"Even to *me*?" Zerah had asked, his eyes widening even more.

"Even to you," his Great Tree had told him, "but not before you become a Great Tree. And then, after you die, you will live on."

"I know," Zerah had replied. "Through my seeds."

"Your memory will live on through your seeds. Your body will live in the earth.

You will then know a new life as earth, and you will nourish another Great Tree. And then you will know life as another Great Tree, for that which nourishes is eternally part of what it has nourished. And on it will go. So when death comes to you, remember that it is nothing to fear. Death is just the process through which our bodies are born again. Death is life in another form."

At that moment, Zerah had felt as though he knew all there was to know about death. But now, lying inside the deep, dark hole, and feeling an even deeper, darker hole within himself, Zerah understood that there was another type of death; one that had nothing to do with memories or the body, but rather with the heart and what lived inside it. He realized that death was more than just an uprooting. It was the understanding that nothing beautiful would ever root itself again.

Zerah's body had been transformed. It had been crushed, but it still existed. There were feelings inside his heart and beliefs inside his mind, however, that were no more.

Once again, Zerah's love for the Wind was gone, and it felt as though the Wind's love for him had never been. Losing the Wind a second time was even more painful than losing it the first. The love that had survived an Uprooted Tree, a changed plan, and a faithless Sidewalk had not survived a human foot.

The Second Grain of Sand considered the Wind cruel; the Little Tree believed it was kind; and the Sidewalk claimed it was speed. For Zerah, the Wind was dead. Not the Wind outside him; the one that partnered with humans' hair, ruffled birds' feathers, and made the tall buildings sway. That Wind lived on. But the Wind within Zerah's heart did not. It bore no beauty. It gave no comfort. It offered no love. Worse still, its remains, as heavy as an uprooted tree, had destroyed his dream. Crushed, dead, and buried: that was the state of Zerah's dream now. After all, could a crushed seed ever become the Greatest Tree? Could he even become a tree at all? And if not, what would become of him?

While growing on his Great Tree, Zerah had heard the same words spoken many times over: "You are... not yet, but you *will* be, my dear little seeds. You will be great one day. You will have big, thick trunks; strong, secure branches; hundreds of leaves;

delicious orange fruit; exquisite, multicolored flowers; and many seeds of your own. You will house the homeless, give rest to the tired, satiate the hungry, add beauty to the world, and ensure your eternal life! You will be important, useful, special, happy, and loved."

"I will be," Zerah had repeated to himself many times over. "I will be important, useful, special, happy, and loved. I will be. I will be. I *will* be!"

Now, Zerah wondered: *What will I be? And if I 'was not' before I was crushed, what have I become? What is less than 'was not'? What is less than 'is not'?*

Death was not an end, but a continuation. At least, that was what Zerah had thought before being crushed. *But a continuation of what?* he asked himself now. *Of my pain? Of my sorrow?*

"Death is just the process by which our bodies are born again," his Great Tree had said. "Death is life in another form."

So where is this life after death my Great Tree spoke of? The leaves become earth, and the earth becomes trees. What can dead faith become? Dead love? A dead dream? Is there a way to make these things live again?

Where is the truth the Little Tree spoke of? The truth he gave me was nothing more than another belief. Does a truth that is always true exist? If I find it, will it make the pain in my heart and head go away? I know nothing can help my body.

There was too much sorrow within Zerah to be contained. His heart pushed his words out into the world of sound. And there, yet again, an embrace called *listening* met his words.

"I was such a foolish seed," he said aloud. "What if I had rooted myself in the desert after having met the Little Tree instead of waiting around for the Wind to teach me my next lesson? There was a moment when I could have done so. I didn't see it then, but I see it now. I could have rooted myself right then and there. If I had, I would never have to answer these questions. If I had, I would never have been crushed."

"Perhaps not," spoke a gentle voice, "but you might have been a tree that was uprooted. Or that got sick. Or that was cut down. Or that was broken, piece by piece, until…" There was a pause, and then the voice became gentler still. "…Until you looked like me. And then you would still be seeking answers, for there are always questions to be answered, and they are always the same questions: Why? How? Where? Who? What? When? No one escapes these questions, no matter where or who they are. Then there is: What if? That's the worst of them. I'm so glad that I don't ask it anymore!"

"Who said that?" Zerah asked.

"Look up," said the voice.

Zerah raised his eyes and saw something partially covering the top of the deep, dark hole.

"Who are you?" asked Zerah.

"I am a twig," said the Twig.

"What is that?" he asked.

He eyed the thin, brown stick above him. She looked familiar.

"Some call me a broken piece of branch. I call myself a Twig."

Zerah looked harder at the Twig and recognized what she was. Zerah had seen other twigs before, lying on the ground. He didn't know how they had ended up there and had never wondered what would become of them. He had thought they were dead, like the fallen leaves, and that there was nothing they could do until they were reborn as soil. Their transformation was so slow and boring that Zerah had never watched it. Now he wondered if they had really died or had just been sleeping.

This Twig is very much alive and awake. And it seems as though she has some kind of purpose. But what could that be?

Through the sliver of light the moon was shining into the deep, dark hole, Zerah could see a broken, jagged edge along the Twig's side. *The break obviously wasn't fatal. Perhaps she has already been reborn. But to be reborn as a twig; what kind of rebirth is that?*

"Who are you?" the Twig asked Zerah, interrupting his thoughts.

"I am Zerah. A crushed seed."

"Crushed is what has been done to you," said the Twig, "but it is *not* who you are."

"Then who am I?" asked Zerah.

"You do not know?" the Twig asked. Sorrow gathered in the next words she said. "Neither do many."

Zerah stared at the Twig, who remained silent for a moment.

Then she breathed in deeply, exhaled fully, and answered Zerah's question. "You are a miracle."

"A miracle?" asked Zerah, confused. "What is that? A type of seed?"

"No," the Twig said, smiling. "It is *every* type of seed. Every speck of soil, blade of grass, grain of sand, animal, human, and insect is a miracle. A miracle is everything and everyone. A miracle is something very great indeed."

"I don't understand," said Zerah.

"Neither do many," the Twig repeated.

Zerah looked down at his crushed body. *There is nothing great about that.* He shifted his gaze to the jagged edge that ran along the Twig's body. When he did, an image of the Uprooted Tree flashed through his mind. All of a sudden, he knew how the twigs had ended up on the ground.

Beliefs affect your eyes and not only your mind and heart, thought Zerah. *I saw without seeing.* Anger welled up within him. It formed a question he already knew the answer to. "The Wind broke you from your tree, didn't it?"

"Well," said the Twig, her words emerging slowly, "the Wind was the one who broke me from my tree when I was still a branch. The second one who broke me—"

"You were broken more than once?" Zerah interrupted.

Being crushed once was horrific enough. Zerah didn't want to imagine the horror of being crushed again. He looked at the Twig more closely. He saw that she didn't only have one jagged edge, but several.

"I have been broken many times. Once by the Wind, once by a car, once by a dog, and more times than I can count by the memory of those breaks inside my heart and mind."

Zerah wondered how many times he had been broken by his memory since he had been crushed by the human's foot. *Yes,* he thought sadly, *I have been crushed many times. Am I such a bad seed? What did I do to deserve this? Am I being punished? If so, for what? For having been impatient with, or cruel to, a grain of sand? But doesn't every seed make mistakes? And if I am being punished, who is punishing me? The Wind? The human? The human stepping on me was an accident; the Wind not coming was intentional.*

Zerah turned to the Twig. "The others broke you accidentally, didn't they?"

The Twig was quiet for a moment before speaking. "The Car that broke me did so intentionally, and with cruelty… with tremendous cruelty… with something called *savagery.*"

"Savagery?" Zerah repeated, his eyes wide, his voice shaking as it uttered the new and frightening word. *"Why?"*

"Because he could," replied the Twig.

"Because he could?" asked Zerah, stunned. "He could have done many things! Why did he do *that*?"

Zerah didn't understand. He wondered how—in a world made up of days stretched long between sunrises and sunsets, days bursting with trees and blades of grass and stars—anyone would want to spend those days breaking others with savagery rather than reveling in beauty. Who wouldn't want to crowd the moments of their lives with bark and its dance of colors: silver in the rain, amber in the sun, black in the shade, brown in the moon? Who would forsake the company of blades of grass, who promised friendship to every fallen leaf, ant, and human that lay upon them; a promise that was always fulfilled? Who would choose to fill their nights with anything but the stars, who never tired of sharing light—as the sun, setting early and rising late; and the moon, three-quarters, a half, a quarter, then disappeared—sometimes did? How could it be that—in a world where everyone lived beholden to the Wind, suffering its whims, trying and failing to end that pain—anyone would decide to increase the suffering of others?

The Twig spoke again. "I have been given many reasons by others. I have been told that the Car was taught to break, and that he believed in that teaching. I have been told that he himself was broken, and that he did to another what had been done to him. I have been told that he felt powerless, so he wanted to exert power over others."

"Those are not reasons to break someone!" Zerah cried out.

"Zerah, reasons are only explanations, not justifications. In the end, there was but one reason why he broke me: it was because he made a choice to break."

Words, which can help rebuild a world that has been destroyed, did no such thing for Zerah. The more the Twig spoke, the less he understood. *A car that felt powerless against a little twig? Didn't he have his own power? Why did he want more? Who could know the pain of being broken and still choose to break another? Who would teach someone to break with intention and savagery? How could it be? Why?*

The deep, dark hole was starting to feel deeper and darker. The little that Zerah could see with his eyes—a single star, a ray of moonlight, and the Twig's jagged edges—disappeared behind an image in his mind. He saw something even crueler than a tree being uprooted by the Wind; more horrible than an oblivious human crushing a seed. He saw the Twig being broken with intention and savagery. His ears filled up with her cries. The loud snap of branches being broken by the Wind, and the almost total quiet of a seed being crushed by a foot became the deafening whack of a branch being severed by a car. That sound echoed many times over in his head and his heart, growing louder each time. He searched for silence but couldn't find it. Shredded bark and splintered wood falling upon the earth, disappearing into the dust as though they had never been, always make a sound. Zerah listened, and he heard it.

The boundary between Zerah's life and the Twig's disappeared, and his heart hurt in response to her pain.

Then fear, slight at first, began to swell, claiming more and more space in Zerah's heart. He soon understood that *takings* existed as well as *offerings*, and he didn't know what power he had over those. Being crushed had taken away Zerah's faith in the Wind. The Car's action, his choice, was taking Zerah's faith in life bit by bit, for life is so deeply connected that the single action of a single being in one time and place affects other beings in other times and places. Every single act of savage breaking breaks many. Every single taking takes much.

Up until that moment, Zerah had questioned what the Wind could or would do. He had wondered when death would come to him. But he had never questioned life. He had never asked whether the soil would make a place for him, or whether the rain would continue to fall. He had never wondered whether the sun would one day stop shining.

Now he wondered about all these things, and more. He wondered about the birds the Sidewalk had said ate seeds. He wondered what it meant to be *swept up*, and what *garbage* was. He realized that the Sidewalk's claims were true, and wondered why he had also chosen savagery. *Does he not know that kindness is a choice, and that he has the power to choose it?*

Zerah thought about the Teeny Beetle and Tiny Mouse. *Are there other creatures who think that differences are wrong and must be punished? Are those creatures big enough to impose punishments? Are there songs that have been silenced? Are there some whose flight patterns have been forced upon them? Are there others who are not permitted to fly at all?*

Zerah wondered whether there were others like the Large Spine who dreamed of scattering; others with legs and wings who could make that dream come true. *Have some beings already been scattered? Have many already been sliced in two?* Zerah considered the Large Spine more carefully. *He is a spine without a tree. Has he already been scattered? Sliced in two himself?* Zerah thought of the Little Tree, who had many spines. *Has the Large Spine been sliced in ten? Or one hundred? Or one thousand? Is he all that's left of a tree? Or of many trees?* Zerah puzzled again at how anyone would want to cause the same harm to others that they themselves had suffered.

Zerah wondered about all the ways one could be broken. He thought about all the beings in the world, each with the potential to break another. He wondered how many creatures had been broken, and how many chose to break.

Zerah thought of the Uprooted Tree and wondered whether the uprooting truly had been a blessing. *Did the pain from the uprooting prevent her from suffering an even worse pain than sickness or being chopped down?* Then he wondered why there had to be sickness at all; why trees had to be cut down; why the Uprooted Tree might have been spared a worse pain, but not the Twig; why anything bad or sad had to happen.

As Zerah questioned life, he questioned death again; not when it would come to him, but why it existed at all, and why it was needed to sustain life. *Trees must die to clear a space for seeds to root themselves. But why?*

Zerah wondered about the first break ever. *How did it come about? Were animals, humans, insects, seeds, and trees to blame? Was it the fault of the Wind? Or was death guilty? Are the Wind and death broken, just like other creatures? If so, how were they broken?*

Zerah wondered if he had ever broken another. *Have I ever been like the human, completely unaware of my actions and their effects? Can some choices be made without realizing what you are choosing?* He pondered whether the fulfillment of some dreams was dependent upon the death of other dreams. *If I turned the desert into a forest, would that mean scattering grains of sand?*

Zerah thought again of the Car, and of intentions. The Second Grain of Sand's words about justice resounded within his heart: "Justice means fairness. Fairness means if you do good things, good things happen to you. And if you do bad things, you face consequences."

"What happened to the Car?" Zerah asked the Twig.

"He drove off," replied the Twig.

"He drove off?" Zerah asked, his eyes widening, his voice rising. "So he faced no consequences?"

The Twig's words emerged at the slow pace of pain that does not want to be said, but knows it has to be. "I do not know if he ultimately faced consequences. Sometimes one faces those a very long time after the hurt they inflicted. But I know that even if he had been broken into a thousand pieces, that would never have returned all that he took from me. And I know that when savagery is committed, and there are no consequences soon after, there are further breaks, deep within the head and heart."

The weight of sorrow and incomprehension crushed Zerah's voice. His words emerged quiet and small. "So you never found justice."

"No," said the Twig. "I did not, though I searched for a very long time. However, I did find that I was not alone in my search for justice."

So the Second Grain of Sand was right. There is no justice; not for those broken by the Wind, or by humans, or by cars.

Zerah looked at the Twig and then surveyed the world around him. Not only did he feel powerless against takings, but suddenly all the trees, blades of grass, and stars seemed less powerful than they had once been. The bark in his mind's eye faded to gray and the blades of grass turned yellow and crumbled. The star above him seemed smaller and further away, its light barely reaching him. Now covered by a cloud, the moon's glow was all but gone. Zerah was left in almost total darkness.

Nothing makes any sense. There is no reason.

Zerah looked around the deep, dark hole, then at the places where the Twig's body had been broken. His voice was barely a whisper. "How can you bear to live in a world without justice?"

The Twig looked directly at Zerah, then gazed up at the stars before turning back to him. She spoke aloud. "I can bear it because, though many things cannot be taken back, power can. I can bear it because seeds and trees and blades of grass and stars exist. I can bear it because, along with the senselessness and savagery, there is the sanity of beauty and love, and if nothing up until now could destroy them, nothing ever will. I can bear it because, though the Car's heart was filled with hatred, my heart is not. The Car may not know who he is, who he *truly* is, but I know who I am."

Zerah was still. He looked up at the star. It felt no closer.

He took a deep breath, let it out, and then asked the Twig, "The Dog who broke you… how did it happen? Intentionally? Cruelly? Savagely?"

The Twig beamed. "Accidentally. Beautifully. Thankfully. Someone had hurled me into the air and she caught me. That was how we met. She loves me, and I love her. It was a very different kind of break."

"*Love* broke you?" asked Zerah, shocked.

"Indeed it did," replied the Twig. "But love, along with knowledge, is what transformed me from a broken branch into a whole twig."

Zerah shook his head. *How could I ever have considered myself a wise seed? I don't understand beautiful breaks, or how knowledge can help make someone whole. Knowledge of what? I don't understand the Wind, or other beings, or power, or death, or life, or love. I am not a wise seed but a terrified one; scared of the Wind, humans, cars, and birds, and of being crushed, swept, and eaten. Perhaps I am even scared of being loved. Yet I need love to become whole. I need love to be.*

The fear that had claimed so much space in Zerah's heart claimed even more. He wondered, *If there is no room for love in a heart filled with hatred, how much space is there for love in a heart filled with fear?*

Zerah said to the Twig, "I'm scared of the Wind and other beings, and death, and love. I'm scared of everything. I'm scared of life!"

"We all are sometimes," the Twig replied. "But remember that you are a part of life. You will find nothing inside your heart that cannot be found in someone else's. Everything and everyone has a heart, Zerah. Remember that. Perhaps it is filled with anger, or pain, or fear, but that doesn't mean it's not a heart. As for hearts that are filled with nothing but hatred, they are far more than broken. They are shattered. They are broken into pieces so small that they are no longer recognizable."

"If the broken can be made whole, can the shattered?" Zerah asked.

"That is the choice of the shattered, and the hope in many hearts."

Hope was the last thing Zerah had in his heart. Anger and pain—much more than he had ever thought it possible for a seed to have; for anyone or anything to have—gripped the walls of his heart and refused to leave. Even more, they pledged to bar joy and peace from entering. With thoughts of the Car came feelings of hatred; a storm battling, raging to be released from dark gray clouds that had taken over the entire sky. Calm blue seemed to have been banished forever. Zerah wanted to break the one who had broken the Twig.

Then he realized that he was too small to do so. He was the same insignificant seed he had always been. There was only one difference now: he was even smaller. And what had been lost—Zerah's faith in the Wind and in life—lay at the bottom of his heart beside what had once been his dream, a flood of grief surrounding them all; the remains of a hurricane.

Even if I can still become a tree, should I? Should I house birds: the birds that eat seeds? Should I provide rest for humans: the humans that crush seeds and steer cars? Or feed mice: the mice that do who knows what to seeds? Should I beautify life? Is life deserving of beauty? Should I perpetuate life? Should life even continue? And if it should, what will I do with my life if I cannot, or do not want to, become a Great Tree? For what purpose was I born, if not to become a Great Tree?

His voice soft, his eyes moist, Zerah asked, "Once you realized that you could never again be what you had been, a branch growing on a tree, what did you do?"

The Twig said, "I didn't do. I only thought. I thought my life was over."

Zerah nodded his head. "And then?"

"And then, one day, I understood that it wasn't; that after death there can be rebirth. And that, just as power can be taken back, joy can be felt again. And then," the Twig paused, and a smile as radiant as a sunrise lit her entire face up with joy, "I did something called *make meaning*."

Make meaning. Zerah repeated the words in his mind. He heard them echo inside his heart. He felt something he hadn't felt since before he had been crushed: the possibility of an answer. Maybe he wouldn't always have to search. Perhaps he wouldn't always be asking *why*. Maybe a truth existed that was always true. Perhaps there was a way to make sense from senselessness.

"You mean you understand why the Wind breaks and why it doesn't stop others from breaking?"

"That is *find meaning*. Some do indeed find it, but I wasn't one of them. *Make meaning* isn't dependent on the Wind's, or anyone else's, heart or actions. It is dependent on your own."

"So what is *make meaning*?" asked Zerah.

The Twig's face glowed like the sun when it was high up in the sky. "It is, first and foremost, a choice. Beyond that, it is many things. It is holding up a camper's tent. That is what I did first, when I was still a branch. I called myself a Support. Make meaning is crossing a desert and climbing a mountain. I called myself a Walking Stick. Make meaning is holding up a bridge over a river. My name was Railing. Then I was broken again, but my ability to make meaning remained intact. I learned that make meaning is also being part of a beaver's dam and a bird's nest. Make meaning is playing with a snake on the plains and causing her to laugh. It is giving form to a kite in a park so he can soar up into the sky. Make meaning is helping broken seeds become whole. Make meaning is preventing savage breaks. Make meaning is using your power to create justice, rather than seeking it. Make meaning is looking up at the stars. It is loving the Dog and being loved by her. The truth is, make meaning is so many things that I cannot say them all. But I can say that, though my name has often changed, I have always remained who I am."

As before, Zerah had not understood many of the things the Twig had said. He didn't know what a *camper's tent* was, nor a *bridge, beaver's dam,* or *kite,* nor a *mountain, river, plains,* or *park.* He didn't know how to prevent savage breaks or create justice, or if he would ever have enough power to do so. He didn't know how the Twig had power to do so. But he knew what a dream was, and he understood some of what the Twig had said.

So if I cannot become a tree, or I no longer want to, I can still become something else. Perhaps I can become a wing to mend a broken butterfly.

Or maybe a petal for a flower that is missing one.

Even if it's not very great, it is surely better to be with someone more broken than yourself than to be broken and alone.

Zerah did not know what he would or could become, but he knew that he would never find out if he continued sitting inside the deep, dark hole. He had to leave the hole, but he didn't know how.

The words of the Second Grain of Sand resounded in Zerah's heart: "I have neither legs like an ant, nor wings like a bird. I cannot even slither like a snake. I am totally dependent upon the Wind to take me places, but the Wind takes me nowhere, except from one part of the desert to another. Tell me, legless, wingless seed, how do you think you can leave the desert, except by the graciousness of the Wind? Yet it was that very *graciousness* that brought you here."

"I wish," Zerah said to the Twig, his voice small and his eyes cast down, "that I had legs like an ant or wings like a bird. Then I would be able to leave this deep, dark hole. But I have neither. I am totally dependent upon the Wind to take me places. Yet look where the Wind has taken me. And look what a human did to me after the Wind brought me here. I wish I was dependent upon no one."

The Twig spoke tenderly. "I have known many ants and many birds. Some ants use their legs only to pace back and forth, and some birds use their wings only to fly in small circles. It is not legs or wings that make us move, but our hearts. Even with legs and wings, most ants and birds find themselves in deep, dark holes at least once in their lives. Having legs and wings doesn't keep us from getting into deep, dark holes. Neither does it get us out of them. As for being dependent upon others, even those with legs and wings are dependent upon others, for nothing is independent of anything else. If the ground rejected the ants' feet, could they walk? If the sky refused space to the birds' wings, could they fly? If a tree denied sustenance to seeds, could they grow? If the soil refused space to seeds, could a tree even exist?"

So I must depend upon the hearts of others instead of upon the heart of the Wind, thought Zerah. He trembled with fear as he imagined depending upon another with a heart like the Sidewalk or the Car. Then Zerah looked up at the Twig and knew there were others with hearts like hers. And he trembled a little less.

THE SUN ROSE and set, giving birth to light and extinguishing it, only to bear and bury light again and again. The moon waxed and waned, speaking of eternity and telling old tales about that which had not yet changed: life and its injustices. Zerah still lay in the deep, dark hole, but the darkness inside him had lightened a little. The Twig's words—gentle, strong, and constant—had served as wings, carrying him out of the solitude his fear and distrust had built.

Zerah realized he wasn't alone in the deep, dark hole. Several blades of grass were growing near him.

Their stories of injustice and pain moved the way music does, creating a connection among all who are touched by what they hear. Though Zerah's body was still, a tenderness stirred within him, silently reclaiming space from the hatred inside his heart. Individual moments disappeared from his mind, leaving one long stretch of time filled with an uninterrupted struggle. Zerah was shocked to find that it wasn't only his life or the Twig's or the Second Grain of Sand's that was unfair; it was life itself that was unfair.

"The Sidewalk was not always the Sidewalk," the First Blade of Grass said. "Once he was specks of soil and rocks. These beings lived alongside us, not above us. They didn't dictate our fate; they shared it. When we were flooded by the rain, they were drenched as well. When we were buried under the snow, they froze beside us. When we were scorched by a blazing sun, they were also burned. We struggled together."

The First Blade of Grass began to cough. Zerah saw that it was no easier for her to breathe inside the deep, dark hole than it was for him. *So this is what the Sidewalk meant by "smother."*

The First Blade of Grass nodded to the Second Blade of Grass, who straightened his back as much as he could, then coughed a little himself. When he was eventually able to speak, he said, "There are four struggles in life. That is the first one: the struggle that cannot be chosen. We cannot choose whether there are rains or floods or droughts. We cannot choose how much the sun shines, or if it doesn't shine at all. We cannot choose whether or not this struggle for light and water exists. It simply does."

"But *why* does it exist?" Zerah asked.

Wheezing slightly, the Second Blade of Grass tried to answer, but he couldn't catch his breath.

The Third Blade of Grass said, "Understanding *why* is the second struggle; the inevitable one. For me, it is also a refuge for hope when despair arrives, clutching a long history of the savagery that has been; demanding that I see only the injustice that is; threatening to take over as the ruler of my mind and heart. We *do* ask *why* there is darkness, hunger, and pain. And in that asking, there is hope."

Hope. After his talks with the Twig, the sound of that word reminded Zerah of the moist soil of his dream; as though the sun was going to find him; as though the sky wouldn't always be out of reach.

"There are many answers to the question why," the Third Blade of Grass continued. "Not one has ever stopped that question from being asked again and again. But there are other questions, all of which start with *how*. They are just as important to ask, and even more important to answer."

Zerah thought of the question starting with *how* that he had once asked: *How do I get to a field so I can root myself and become a Great Tree?* It had once been his only question. Now it was but one of a multitude. He couldn't answer any of them, and he couldn't stop asking why.

"Why did some specks of soil and rocks change?"

The Third Blade of Grass leaned over to gasp for air. The Fourth Blade of Grass spoke. "Teachings."

Zerah's eyes grew large. "Teachings? What kind of teachings?"

"Savage teachings." The Fourth Blade of Grass shuddered. He closed his eyes, but that shut out nothing. Memory, both burden and blessing, dispatched liquid pain to his eyes. Tears fell soundlessly, disappearing into the ground as though they had never been. But they had been. And some silences must be said.

The Fourth Blade of Grass opened his eyes. He spoke slowly, raising his words up from the grave where the Sidewalk had tried to bury the truth alongside the smothered.

"Zerah, there is a difference between choosing to value life and choosing to value only *your* life. There arose savage teachings which said, 'Only your own life matters.' Some specks of soil and rocks believed them. They desired to implement them. But no one can survive alone, so they united with others who believed the same teachings."

"So the Sidewalk doesn't smother you just because you are blades of grass?"

The Fourth Blade of Grass cringed. "I have heard such things many times. I have heard that twigs are broken with savagery because they asked to be broken. I have heard that if I were a jagged rock rather than a blade of grass, the Sidewalk wouldn't hurt me. I have even heard it said that seeds must be crushed in order to teach them kindness. My heart breaks every time I hear such words, for words can break as much as cars and sidewalks. No creature *ever* asks to be broken with savagery. No seed *ever* deserves to be crushed. No blade of grass has *ever* been smothered just for being a blade of grass. If that were so, I would need to become something other than what I am—something other than a blade of grass—to prevent savagery. Blades of grass are smothered, twigs are broken with savagery, and seeds are told they deserve to be crushed because of the beliefs of those who do and say these things."

Words, which can help rebuild a world that has been destroyed, began to erect new ideas within Zerah, creating connections between the disparate and building bridges across distances. *So beliefs come from teachings, and savage teachings are one of the reasons for injustice and pain. Injustice takes many forms: scatterings, breakings, smotherings. Injustices occur in many places: deserts, cities, deep, dark holes. Those who suffer such injustices have many shapes: grains of sand, twigs, blades of grass. But in the end, it is all the same savagery. It is the same teaching.*

Zerah thought of the stars, which shared their light equally with all. *With teachers like that, how could any savage teachings ever come to be?* He asked the Fourth Blade of Grass.

The Fifth Blade of Grass spoke after the Fourth Blade of Grass, eyes watering, back bent, nodded to her to continue.

"Fear."

"Fear of what?" Zerah asked.

"Fear of power."

Zerah thought of the Car again. "I don't understand," he said. "Why would anyone fear power? I was once told that every single one of us has our own power."

The fifth Blade of Grass nodded. "And that is exactly why those who became the Sidewalk were—and still are—afraid, because the Wind, sun, rains, animals, humans, and insects all have power as well. The Wind can scatter, the sun can burn, the rains can flood, the animals can scatter, the humans can burn, and the insects can break, with cruelty as much as with love. Our paths can be altered by others. Our deaths can be decreed by others. The more powerless you feel with regard to your own life, the more power you try to take from others' lives. The more power you have taken, the more you fear losing it. And the more savagery you will commit to prevent losing it.

"That fear, that feeling of powerlessness, gave rise to the third struggle in life: the one that should never exist. Some specks of soil and rocks clustered together, so tightly that no one could pass between them. The specks of soil had turned hard, and the sweetness within their hearts had become rotten, harsh, and sour. The rocks could have broken with great love into tender specks of soil or gentle grains of sand, for those in fields and deserts and cities originate from the same source. Instead, they had chosen to fracture into jagged pieces that cut and scar. They looked more like shattered hearts than rocks. They had all become something they were never meant to be. We no longer all helped each other."

The Fifth Blade of Grass lowered her head, her body aching.

The First Blade of Grass, still breathing with difficulty, continued. "Now life is such that even on days when the sun shines, we do not all feel it. Even when the rain is constant and gentle, we do not all know it. We cannot all see the stars. We have grown yellow instead of green. We are brittle instead of soft. Some of us couldn't bend, so…" She paused. Grief offered up words too small to describe such massive pain. "We broke." Tears clouded her eyes. "And some of us," her voice faltered, "were born and died faster than the time it takes to speak the prayer, 'Grow.' We do not struggle to thrive, or even live; we struggle to survive."

Rage at the injustice of it all took possession of Zerah's heart once again. Then, awe at the strength of the blades of grass lit his eyes with the same wonder the stars did. *How can those who have been denied the stars' light still have so much light within them? How can those who are barely able to breathe find the strength to continue breathing?*

"But despite everything, you survive," said Zerah.

"We do," said the First Blade of Grass, her shallow breaths slowly becoming deeper. "So many of us have died, smothered by savagery. But our desire to live hasn't, though at times it is a struggle to maintain it. It is the fourth struggle: the one we must choose. The one we must choose again and again, because in every moment we make a choice, and in every moment we can make a different choice."

"And what is the struggle that we must choose? Is it the struggle to live despite the Sidewalk?" Zerah asked.

"It is the struggle to change," said the Second Blade of Grass. His breaths, though still uneven, were a little fuller.

"To change what?" asked Zerah.

"To change many things," said the Third Blade of Grass, her voice a little stronger than before. "Some say it is to change the Sidewalk so that he returns to who he once was. I say it is to change who has our power—it is to *take back* our power—so that we can become who we deserve to be; who we were born to be: green and soft. Ultimately, it is to change savage beliefs and teachings. It is to change hearts and minds."

Zerah beheld the blades of grass in amazement once again. *How can those who have suffered such ugliness choose such beauty? They are so strong! Despite all the power he has taken, the Sidewalk is so weak.*

And yet…

Footsteps pounded above Zerah's head. The Sidewalk's voice thundered within the deep, dark hole. The blades of grass were almost as pale as grains of sand. Zerah considered how impenetrable the Sidewalk seemed; how deeply the blades of grass ached; how difficult it had been for him to change his beliefs about the Wind, which had come from teachings; how difficult it was for him to change anything.

"It is not an easy struggle to change," said Zerah.

"No," replied the Fourth Blade of Grass, his eyes still watering and back still bent. "It is not."

"There are only five of you. It will be even harder because you struggle alone."

In that moment, a chorus of specks of soil—more numerous than the stars in the sky, louder than the birds and cicadas in a field, louder than the owls, crickets, and bees in a desert, louder even than the Wind when its voice stretched across time and space, connecting yesterday to today and today to tomorrow, uniting the clouds with the earthworms, serving as a teacher for the divided, pledging, proving, "With unity, this is what you can do" —sang back, "They are not alone." They moved a little closer to Zerah and sang again, "No one is alone."

Then the ground beneath Zerah shook, and the deep, dark hole got a little wider, letting in a little more light. Zerah finally understood how the Twig could create justice: by not being alone.

He looked around him. The specks of soil far outnumbered the Sidewalk, yet the Sidewalk stood firm, seemingly unalterable.

Zerah spoke to the blades of grass. "Even with so many, it is still difficult. Do you never tire of struggling?"

"Of course we do," said the Fourth Blade of Grass. "But once you answer the question, 'What makes the struggle worthwhile?' you are able to continue, even when you think you have no strength left inside you to do so."

His back straightened, and the Fifth Blade of Grass stood so tall that Zerah could no longer see the top of her.

Zerah couldn't get his words out quickly enough, "What is the answer?"

"*The* answer?" grinned the First Blade of Grass. "It is different for everyone. For me, it is my dream of knowing the rain and sun and moon and stars in my life; not only when I sleep, or through someone else's memories."

Zerah looked all around him at the other blades of grass, specks of soil, and the Twig, who still lay above him, her eyes as bright as the sun's.

"And for you?" Zerah asked them all.

"My dream," said the Second Blade of Grass, "is to feel the Wind upon me."

"My dream," said the Third Blade of Grass, "is to see soft earth and smooth rocks all around me."

"My dream," said the Fourth Blade of Grass, "is to watch small blades of grass grow tall."

"My dream," said the Fifth Blade of Grass, "is to have flowers growing beside me."

"Our dream," spoke the specks of soil, "is to welcome our sisters and brothers home."

"My dream," said the Twig, "is to make meaning."

Between the sounds of steps above his head, Zerah heard a human's voice: "My dream is to be embraced by other humans."

What about my dream? Zerah asked himself. It was in this moment that he felt something moving in his heart. With trepidation, he looked inside it. Was it anger that was stirring within him? Pain? Fear? Zerah was shocked to find that it was none of these things. It was his dream rousing; it wasn't dead after all. It had been broken but not destroyed. And now, it was awake. As in the desert, Zerah had grown. Only this time, not only had his mind and heart grown, but so had his body. From beneath him sprouted a single, tiny, sturdy root.

Zerah could still become a tree. Part of him had been crushed, but his dream had not.

"I can become a tree!" Zerah called out, a deep joy stretching his words so wide that even a bird in the sky heard them. "I *will* become a tree! And I will be important and useful and special and happy! I will be loved!"

"But," Zerah vowed, "I will *not* be a tree here in this deep, dark hole. I will be one in a field!"

That very afternoon, Zerah emerged into the light. His heart had indeed moved him, but so had the hearts of the Twig, the blades of grass, the specks of soil, and four passing ants, who became his legs and carried him out of the deep, dark hole.

A FIELD. ZERAH saw it in his mind's eye. He saw blades of grass to his left and his right; before him and behind him. They were too many to count, standing tall and green. They were as beautiful as the view above him: the sky, clear and blue. It was only a matter of time before it would be within reach. Below him was reddish-brown earth, soft and moist; a place where his body could rest even if his mind, still searching, could not.

Savagery exists, but so does kindness. The Wind exists, but so do legs and wings. Instead of depending on the Wind, I will depend on others; those who have hearts like the Twig and the blades of grass and the specks of soil and the ants. And I will go to a field and root myself!

The path to a field finally seemed easy and straight, but the more Zerah thought about his arrival there, the more the field in his mind changed. It narrowed and shrunk, again and again, until the blades of grass were too thin to see, and the reddish-brown earth became a single speck of soil. In their place was the sky, the names of all the corners of the world the Twig had visited, and the wonder of how many other places existed. Zerah saw the enormity of what he had never seen: life beyond a field, desert, and city. He asked himself the question he had asked before: *What is there in life that I don't know?* The existence of his root and the certainty that his dream would now come true transformed his fear into curiosity, and the unknown suddenly didn't seem so scary.

Perhaps there's a place that is even better than a field! After all, if my Great Tree was wrong about the Wind, he may also have been wrong about the field.

Boundaries Zerah hadn't realized existed suddenly burst open. Limited knowledge no longer seemed like knowledge. He reasoned that as he had needed to speak to many grains of sand in order to know the desert, so too would he have to visit many places in order to know where to root himself. The deep, dark hole in his past was replaced with a future that was as brightly lit as a sunrise accompanied by the lights of the night; sun, moon, and stars, all gleaming together, ready to illuminate the numerous places on earth where Zerah could root himself.

Aside from the *cannot choose* and the *must choose* there was the *could choose*, and it was vast. It was so vast that his journey would stretch wide across time, and he would move from wonder to wonder until his eyes had the same knowledge of the earth as the sky. It was so vast that perhaps even a hundred lifetimes might not be enough to experience every possible choice. It was so vast that Zerah's wonder soon became weariness, his life an endless search for the best place to root himself without ever doing so. *And then,* he thought sadly, *at the end of my life I will still be exactly what I was when I began it.*

Zerah thought of the other seeds that had grown beside him on his Great Tree. *They are probably all Great Trees by now!* he guessed. He could see them clearly: their exquisite, dark trunks, strong enough to withstand any storm; their thick branches reaching so high into the sky that they had befriended the clouds; their leaves more numerous than the stars in the sky; their fruit sweet enough to overpower the bitterness in any heart; their flowers so beautiful that even the speedy humans would slow to a snail's pace in order to gaze upon them; their seeds so plentiful that they could turn hundreds of cities into forests. Most of all, he envisioned the seeds who had grown beside him surrounded by so many who loved them that the meaning of the word *loneliness* had been completely forgotten.

Jealousy and bitterness sought space within Zerah's heart, and they found it. *I bet the Wind never blew them anywhere they didn't want to go! I bet no one ever crushed them!* Then, remembering not only the other seeds, but also the great struggles of so many, shame flushed his face. By the time the color drained, thoughts of Semeeya had filled his head, worry had filled his heart, and tears had begun to gather at the corners of his eyes. *I wonder if the Wind ever blew her anywhere she didn't want to go. I wonder if she has been crushed. I wonder if she is a Great Tree, or if she is still just a little seed like me, wandering this world.*

Zerah swallowed his tears.

He thought of the blades of grass and wondered if a *should choose* existed. *Should I stay in the city and join them in their struggle against the Sidewalk? Is their struggle mine? Is my struggle theirs?*

"Who's to say what you should be doing, anyway? *You* are to say!" the First Grain of Sand had told Zerah.

I say… Zerah paused. He thought of all the places the Twig had told him about. *Mountain* sounded more wondrous than any other.

"A mountain is a very high place," she had said during one of their many conversations. "From the top of it, you can see the world."

A mountain, Zerah decided. *I will go to a mountain. From there I will see the world. I will spot the place I like the best. I will go there and root myself. And then, finally, my dream will come true.*

The corners of Zerah's mouth turned up towards the sky his future branches and leaves would soon know, and the tears of sorrow he had refused to shed found their way into the corners of his eyes in another form: joy.

Zerah spoke to the ants that had carried him out of the deep, dark hole, "Can you take me to a mountain?"

"Why?" the First Ant asked.

"When?" the Second Ant responded.

"Where is it?" the Third Ant questioned.

"What's a mountain?" the Fourth Ant asked.

Zerah rolled his eyes.

Then a voice said, "I can take you to a mountain. I am going to one myself."

"Who said that?" asked Zerah.

"I did. I am a bird," said the Bird.

Zerah looked up to see a bird in front of him. His eyes grew large and his words—"Birds eat seeds"—emerged shakily and softly. They were too soft for the Bird to hear, but loud enough that someone else did.

"Not all birds eat seeds," a voice just as soft as Zerah's said in response.

"Who said that?" asked Zerah.

"I did," said the voice.

"And who are you?" he asked, looking around.

After hearing a "Down here!" Zerah looked down.

"I am a crack in the sidewalk," said the Crack in the Sidewalk with great kindness.

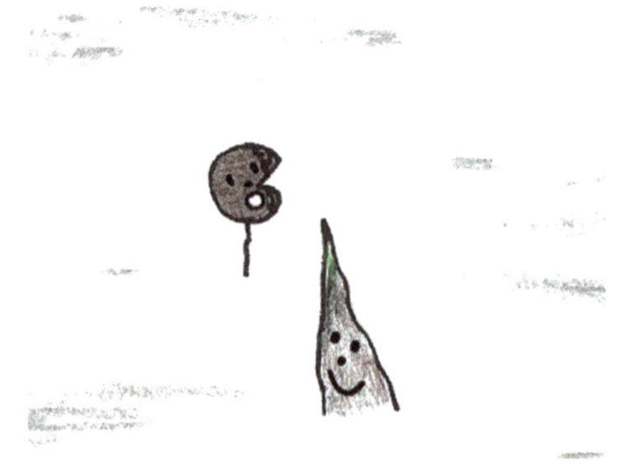

"Who are you?"

"I am Zerah. A scared seed."

"If you are what you feel," said the Crack in the Sidewalk with a laugh, "I must be a mighty crack!" He laughed again and grew a little bigger.

"I don't know if I am what I feel, but I know that I am afraid of what will happen to me if I go with the Bird."

"And what will happen if you don't?" the Crack in the Sidewalk asked.

Zerah thought for a moment. The days to come would be filled with waiting and hoping: waiting for ants who knew the path to a mountain to arrive, and hoping they would be as generous as the ones he had already met; waiting for the inevitable return of the Wind, and hoping it would do him no further harm; waiting for the Sidewalk to direct the speedy humans to the out-of-the-way spot where he now sat, and hoping they would slow down and watch where they stepped. All of a sudden, waiting did what it often does. It transformed hope into despair.

Zerah said, "If I could just know who the Bird was in the past, and whether or not he has eaten seeds, I would know if I should trust him. If I knew what was inside his heart, I wouldn't be afraid."

At that moment, the ground beneath Zerah shook a second time. Still busy directing the humans, the Sidewalk didn't notice. When Zerah looked at the Crack in the Sidewalk, he saw that he had grown bigger again.

"Knowing who someone was in the past won't necessarily tell you who they are now," said the Crack in the Sidewalk. "And knowing who someone is in the present doesn't necessarily tell you who they will become in the future. As for trusting others' hearts, that becomes easier when you trust your own."

Zerah reeled at the thought of trusting his heart. It was easier to trust the Twig's heart, as she had always offered him kindness, than to trust his own. His was brave one moment and scared the next. It was angry, sad and jealous; a mix of so many feelings he was never sure what he would find. There was only one real certainty when it came to his heart: the feeling that he was still nothing.

But it didn't have to be that way. There was a bird before him. A bird with the power to either eat him or to replace nothing with something great. A bird with the power to help him become a Great Tree. There was a quiet voice inside him saying, *Not all birds eat seeds,* and an even quieter voice, so quiet that it sounded like his imagination; so quiet that a whisper would have been like thunder in comparison, telling him, *You can trust this Bird.*

Zerah asked the Crack in the Sidewalk, "How many times must I conquer the same fear?"

The Crack in the Sidewalk answered, "As many times as it arises."

"What makes a fear conquerable?"

"Courage."

"And how does one acquire courage?"

"By conquering one's fears."

Zerah gulped. *Could trusting the Bird's heart really be much more dangerous than trusting the Wind's? Could leaving be worse than staying? Don't I have to risk death to truly live? Besides, even if I die, birth always follows death.*

Always. The instant this word arrived like a sunrise, *not always* followed like a permanent sunset, swallowing the light of the moon and stars as it made its way into total darkness. Zerah wondered whether the other twigs—the ones that had lain motionless below his Great Tree, broken by the Wind and by others; the ones that had never moved or spoken—had been sleeping, or whether there had simply been no rebirth for them.

Zerah addressed Life directly, "Is it possible that birth doesn't always follow death? Are there some who are broken who never become whole, and some who die and never live again? Please, don't let that be me."

"That is not only Life's choice. It is also your heart's."

Zerah looked beside him. There was the Twig. When he first met her, he had thought that she was as weak as he was. Now he aspired to be as strong as her.

He said softly, "Before being crushed, I wasn't as strong as I am now. You made me strong. If I'm crushed again, I don't know if I'll become stronger again, or weaker. Can you give me more strength?"

The Twig's eyes were as clear and bright and beautiful as they had always been. When she looked at Zerah, all he saw was light. "Strength is never given; it is only discovered. Before being crushed, you didn't know how strong you were. I gave you knowledge, not strength. You have all the strength you will ever need inside you. Others can only show, teach, and remind you—for we all need to be reminded at times—of what you already have."

The Twig smiled at Zerah, and Zerah smiled at the Twig.

Then Zerah said, "I need to… I want to go."

"I know," said the Twig.

"I'll miss you," he said, his tears falling into the deep, dark hole in the Sidewalk. The First Blade of Grass turned green and reached up towards the sun.

"I'll miss you, too," said the Twig.

Her tears made the hard earth beneath her moist. The Second Blade of Grass was nourished. He stood tall, a small, soft breeze caressed him, and his yellow body swallowed some blue from the sky.

"I don't know if I'll ever see you again," sniffed Zerah.

"Of course you'll see me again," said the Twig soothingly.

"Where?" he asked.

"Inside your heart," she replied.

Zerah fell silent. *If I look inside my heart to see the Twig, I will also see the empty space beside me where she used to dwell.* He shed another tear. The earth became moist enough for the Third Blade of Grass to rise above the deep, dark hole and reap the benefits of the sun, whose golden light once again performed the magic of making things green.

"Can you come with me?" Zerah asked the Twig. "You'd like to see a mountain again, wouldn't you? It'll be fun! We'll keep each other company on the journey. And if either of us becomes fearful of all the what-ifs as the Bird flies towards the mountain, we'll have the other to remind us not to ask such questions."

He gazed at the Twig, waiting hopefully for her response.

A sweet smile spread across her face. "But the Dog is waiting for me, and probably asking many what-ifs of her own."

Zerah nodded, and his eyes looked upon her with the same tenderness she had always offered him.

When Zerah turned toward the blades of grass, specks of soil, and ants to say goodbye, he was shocked at how hard it was to do so. Within the deepest, darkest hole he had found the brightest, most expansive light. He tried to assemble, from the mass of words inside him, sentences beautiful enough to thank them for what they had done for him. He could not do it. No matter how exquisite, words can only touch the edges of love, never its core. Only a quiet "Thank you," emerged. Many other "thank yous" were offered to him in response, but Zerah did not know why.

Then the Bird picked Zerah up, looked straight ahead, flapped his wings, and soared into the sky. Zerah looked behind him. As he watched the Twig, blades of grass, specks of soil, and ants all grow smaller and smaller, he realized how large a space they had filled inside his heart. The moment they were out of sight, longing seized space within him. His eyes saw absence. His ears heard the gaping silence loving voices often leave behind them when spirits know fullness but ears emptiness; songs within hearts that yearn for but are not reunited with their composers. His mind felt heavy with the impossible task of trying to extricate love from pain. *Yes*, thought Zerah. *Love does break you.*

Zerah didn't understand how this ache would one day help to make him whole, but he guessed that once he had the love of the entire world—a love too large to fit inside a heart; a love powerful enough to uproot anger, pain, fear, sorrow, hatred, loneliness, and nothingness; the love in the dreams of little seeds and the reality of Great Trees—he would be whole. Until then, he decided to think only of the love that was to come rather than feel the love that already existed. Within the depths of Zerah's heart, in the shadows of forgetfulness, in the place where memories could not reach, he did his best to bury the love of the Twig, the blades of grass, the specks of soil, and the ants. Beside their love, slumbered Semeeya's; the fate of her love a model for the fate of theirs: hushed to sleep and then back to sleep whenever it awakened; powerless to hurt but powerless to help.

Zerah turned his head, looked straight ahead, and waited for the mountain to come into view.

HELD FIRMLY BUT gently in the Bird's beak, Zerah soared through the sky.

He passed over the city, then the fields, and then the desert. They didn't appear to be the same city, fields, and desert as before. Zerah couldn't believe how many things he saw differently due to a single human's action and the Wind's inaction.

Life is not what I once believed it to be. Like trees, dreams can die and be reborn. A purpose can be a choice. One can make rather than wait. A twig can be the sun. Blades of grass can be stars. Unity can exclude or include. Takings exist, but so do taking backs. A heart can be legs. A seed can have wings as well as roots. A life can be lived, even if Life itself is not understood.

As Zerah and the Bird flew towards the mountain, the sun set and rose; a promise of the perpetual return of light upon his lips. The moon waxed and waned, speaking of eternity and telling old tales about that which would never change: the struggles, and the dreams that made the struggles worthwhile. Echoes of cries of pain filled up the air like leaves blowing without direction, seeking a life that was no more. But louder, much louder, were the snippets of songs: notes that left long trails of sound behind them, assuring Zerah that there was more music in the world than could ever be heard. All the lyrics were questions. Every answer was a dance, the movements of which had nothing in common but for one motion: a reach towards the future. Zerah watched as his dream, his answer, danced within his heart. His future roots spread, his trunk's rings spiraled, his branches curled, his leaves swayed, his fruit swelled, his flowers fluttered, and his seeds swung freely.

Then the mountain came into view; that is, the *mountains*, for there were many of them! To Zerah's left and right, before him and behind him, he saw exquisite mountains the color of tree trunks, covered with snow the color of the stars. Beneath him was the most beautiful mountain of them all.

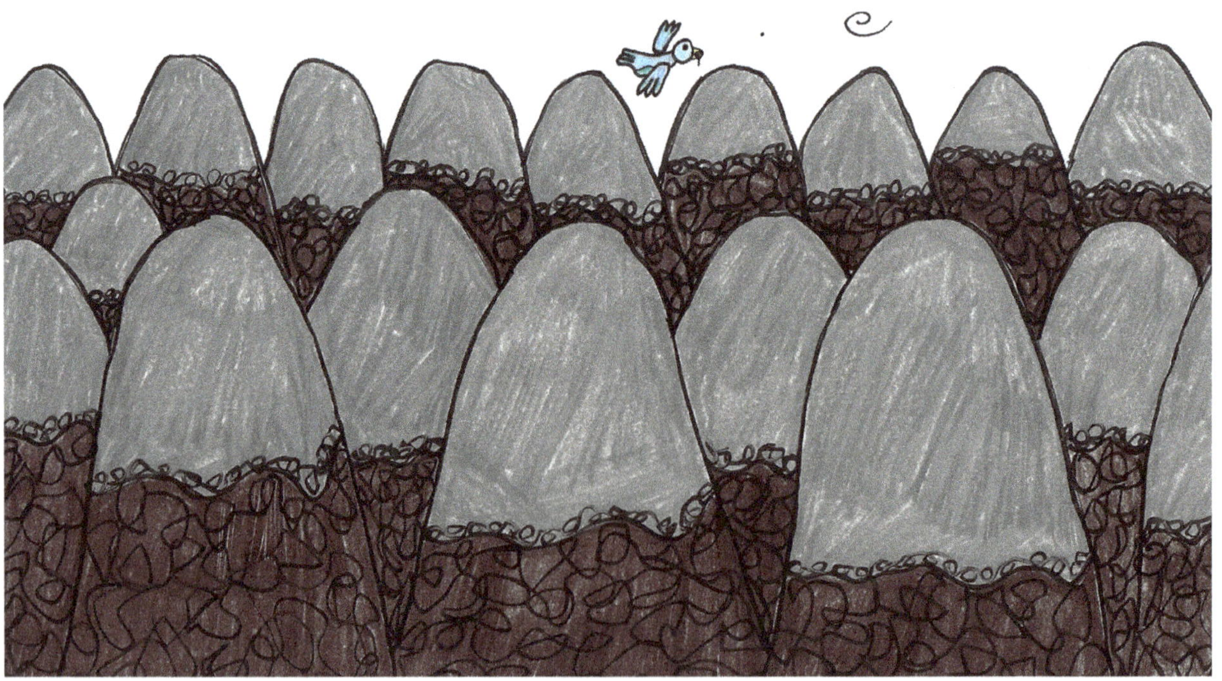

Zerah beamed. *Perhaps I shall root myself here.* For a fleeting moment, everything that had happened in Zerah's life up to that point seemed almost justifiable because it had all led him there: to the Greatest Mountain, where he would become the Greatest Tree. Zerah felt so happy, he decided to sing a variation of the Little Tree's *Wind Song*, which he called *Bird Song*.

Then, out of the corner of his eye, the Bird saw a speck of dust floating in the Wind. With his eyes settled on the speck of dust, he didn't see the bee flying toward him, drunk from too much pollen and zig-zagging through the sky. The Bird and the bee collided, and Zerah fell from the Bird's mouth to the left, while the Bird, tangled in the sky with the bee, fell to the right.

"Zerah!" the Bird cried.

"Bird!" cried Zerah.

But they soon lost sight of each other.

Zerah plummeted towards the earth. He pinched his eyes closed and tried to prepare himself for the breaks that would soon fracture his body into too many pieces to count. Instead, he landed on something soft. Nothing broke. Nothing even hurt.

He opened his eyes and looked around. To his left were mountains! To his right, mountains! Before him and behind him, more mountains! *For joy!* This time, nothing had been ruined, at least, not for Zerah. This time, everything would work out exactly as he had planned. Zerah had almost begun to sing a song to Life when he realized that, beneath him, the spot in which he was sitting, was not a mountain. But what on earth was it?

"Where am I?" Zerah asked aloud.

"You're inside me!" said a hopeful voice.

"Who are you?" asked Zerah.

"I'm a valley!" exclaimed the Valley. "Who are you?"

"I'm Zerah. And I'm trying to get to the top of a mountain."

The Valley let out a small sigh. "So is everyone who comes this way. Instead of setting off, why don't you stay?"

Zerah was stunned. "So I'm not the first to fall?"

The corners of the Valley's mouth turned down towards the earth. "You are not the first, and you will not be the last. In the future, I already see the past. Stay."

Sympathy flooded Zerah's heart. *No wonder the Valley looks so sad. I would also be sad if all I saw in my future was my past.* Then curiosity rained down questions inside Zerah's mind. *Who are the others that have fallen? Seeds? Seeds that I know? Are some of them not Great Trees yet? Or many of them? The Second Grain of Sand told me that others had been blown into the desert. Had they also been seeds?*

Zerah thought of the Twig's words: "You will find nothing inside your heart that cannot be found in someone else's."

This truth had frightened Zerah. If the hatred in his heart was the same as the hatred in the Sidewalk's and the Car's, he worried that he might become like them.

But the same truth in different circumstances can feel like a different truth. A new feeling, one of relief, tunneled its way from Zerah's head to his heart. It was a strange feeling. It wasn't joy derived from another's suffering, or jealousy laid happily to rest. Nor was it his imagination on a dark path, trudging further and further into Semeeya's possible pain.

Relief was the knowledge that other seeds had quite possibly been exactly where he was now, feeling exactly what he felt now. When Zerah considered again what his life might be like compared with the lives of other seeds, he did not find the uniqueness he had long craved, but the commonality he needed to silence the thought: *It's not just that you have done nothing great with your life yet. It's that you are the only seed who hasn't.*

Zerah said to the Valley, "Those who came to the mountains before me, were they seeds seeking the best place to root themselves?"

Sorrow brought the Valley's words as low as his hope had raised them up. "Those who come here are seeking many things, and the love they think those things will bring: triumph through competition, immortal recognition, the fulfillment of others' expectations, and constant validation."

Zerah didn't know if other seeds sought these things. He didn't even know what they were. But he imagined that a view from the mountains was needed to find them.

He said, "I am seeking none of these things. I only want to see where the best place to root myself might be."

The Valley said, "From within me, there is also a view. I can show you where to root yourself, too. Stay."

Zerah was silent for a moment, unsure how to respond without hurting the Valley's feelings. It would have been better to root himself in the desert, or even in the deep, dark hole—where at least he would have had the company of wise and gracious grains of sand, indomitable blades of grass, and courageous specks of soil— than in this Valley, whose words sounded sadder every time he spoke.

Zerah said as gently as he could, "I'm sure the view from inside you is nice, but only the mountains can show me what I need to see."

The Valley nodded. "Yes, of course the view from above is what you wish to see: the great beyond; life as a tree. From far away, all is golden and bright, but up close, if you look hard enough, you will also see light. Stay with me."

Zerah was beginning to lose patience. The mountains were calling to him, singing to him, begging him to accept their offerings, and the Valley was telling him not to listen.

"Valley, I'm sure you mean well, but it has taken a great deal of time for me to get here. Had I not fallen, I would be at the top by now. I'm sorry, but I really have to go."

Eyes wide, the Valley looked at Zerah and said:

The steep climb;
it's a struggle to become.
If not climbed with the essential,
you will forsake everyone.
In the name of the Wind
I've heard many teachings savage.
In the name of greatness
I've seen many lives ravaged.
Houses built by taking,
rest achieved by breaking,
satiation reaped from starvation;
beauty battered, the present moment shattered.
I've seen lives laid side by side
only in an effort to judge,
whose achievements should guarantee them
worthiness and love.
From below looking up, it may be hard to see
that there is already greatness within thee.
The heights can show distance,
and it's beautiful, it's true,
but the depths can see the depths;
you are more than what you have and do.
Remain with me and I will help you see,
who you truly are,
and have the power to be.

Zerah eyed the Valley, then looked again at the mountains. He considered whether to choose incomprehensible rhymes or the steep climb. For once, the answer was easy.

Zerah spoke firmly. "Valley, I'm going to go."

A tear fell from one of the Valley's eyes as he responded sadly with, "I know." Then he remained silent.

Zerah took a deep breath. He reminded himself that he was strong. He reminded himself that, if the Grains of Sand, Little Tree, Twig, Blades of Grass, Specks of Soil, Ants, and Bird he had met existed, surely there were others like them. Once again, Zerah reached out to those around him. Once again, he found many who offered to help.

To Zerah's great surprise, he also found that his journey up the mountain was no more direct than his attempts to journey to a field had been. The days and nights spent climbing were full of pauses and stops, impatience and frustration, like a field forever in sight but forever out of reach.

"Wow! Look how much beauty there is to see! Before we get started, let's stop and look around for a while," said Zerah's first traveling companion, the Rabbit with insatiable eyes who moved more slowly than a snail.

He had hopped over to Zerah in the Valley. After that, the word *amble* better described his movements.

"Want to see how fast I can move? Faster than a rabbit!" said the Snail with whom Zerah traveled next. The Snail proceeded to dig herself into a hole, which took many sunsets and sunrises to escape from.

"Forward isn't always so great. Let's go backward!" exclaimed Zerah's third travel partner, the Snake who wound up leaving Zerah at the base of the mountain.

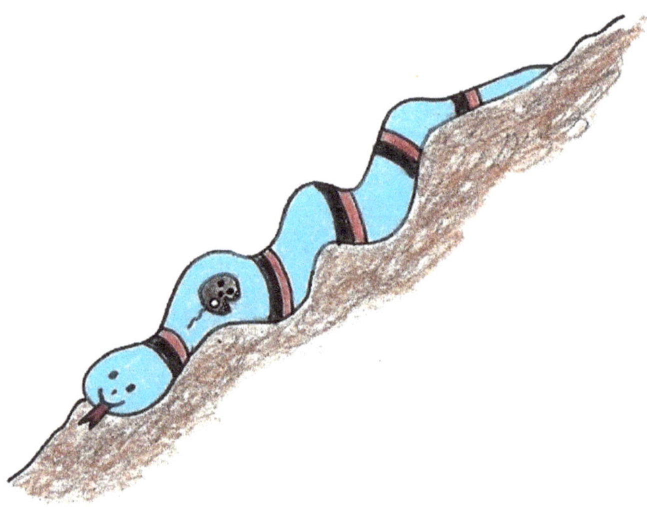

As Zerah's time on the mountain lengthened, and the many additional travel companions he met moved in much the same way as the first three, he wondered if he would be climbing up the same small section of the mountain for the rest of his days.

Other times, Zerah wondered if he would ever climb anywhere at all, for there were plenty of creatures like his thirteenth companion, the Dragonfly who didn't travel slowly, or in circles, or backward. He simply didn't move. He sat still and chatted with his friends: the crickets, the stones, and the clouds.

When Zerah urged the Dragonfly to move on, he urged Zerah to be still.

"Don't you have a destination to reach?" Zerah asked.

The Dragonfly gestured towards his friends and said, "I have already reached it." Then he asked Zerah, "Would you like to stay with us?"

Zerah declined and continued his climb upwards with the Ladybug who reminded him of the Little Tree.

"Dear Zerah," she said. "How can you think you are moving too slowly when you have complained to me about the humans who move too quickly? Have faith. You will reach the mountaintop."

As Zerah journeyed on, he also crossed paths with those who reminded him of the Sidewalk. There was the Plastic Bag who vowed to smother everyone, causing the bee on whose back Zerah was riding to tear away, buzzing in panic.

Then there was the Metal Tube with a booming voice that made the chipmunk he was traveling with flee into a burrow.

This time, Zerah felt not only the fear in his heart, but also the fear in the hearts of those with whom he traveled, their bodies shaking beneath him. To his great astonishment, he also saw fear when he looked into the eyes of the Plastic Bag and the Metal Tube.

Still he journeyed on.

In addition to the legs, wings, beaks, backs, kindness, and time Zerah's travelling companions offered him, they shared the stories of their lives. He, in turn, listened. The stories were as different as the grains of sand, but each had this in common: there was always a struggle, and always a dream that made the struggle worthwhile. It soon seemed to Zerah that there were not four struggles in life but many; every single one connected to a dream that was as difficult to fulfill as his own.

"I dream of being soft," said the Beetle.

"I dream of being hard," said the Rabbit.

"I dream of having wings," said the Bush.

"I dream of having roots," said the Bee.

"I dream of flying the highest," said the Bird.

"I dream of digging the deepest," said the Chipmunk.

"I dream of space," said the Newborn Butterfly.

"I dream of time," said the Dying Ant.

Time, thought Zerah. *That is the only thing I have aside from my dream, a mind that still doesn't understand many things, and a heart and body that are still broken.*

Zerah had once counted sunrises and sunsets. Now he counted moments. They left as fast as they arrived. He didn't know why the present had a name. No sooner did the future deliver time to him than the past snatched it away. Once gone, these moments could never be taken back. Zerah thought again of the speedy humans. Perhaps they hadn't only been following the Sidewalk's orders. Perhaps they had been rushing to fulfill their dreams before their time ran out.

How much time do I have left in this one life I'm living to fulfill my dream before death comes again? Why do some receive so much time, and others so little? Is this another reason why others break? Do they think they have such an abundance of time that no

Urgency set the speed and tone of Zerah's speech as he climbed further and further up the mountain. He begged every slow traveling companion to move quickly, and every swift traveling companion to move more swiftly.

There were, however, occasional moments when he wanted to pause, or even stop traveling completely. One morning, Zerah found a purple patch of earth on the side of the mountain. For a brief instant, he wanted to root himself there and then.

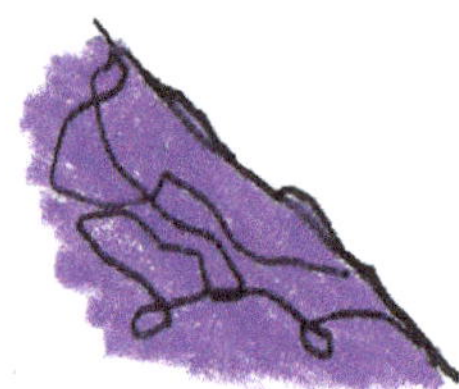

One afternoon, a cloud covered the heat of the sun and Zerah wanted to cool off in his shade.

One evening, there was a rain shower, whose quiet patter silenced the questions in Zerah's head. He wanted to rest beneath those drops.

There was a puddle Zerah wanted to drink from.

There was a birdsong he wanted to hear.

And then, late one night, he encountered a rock he wanted to lie upon; a rock that wanted Zerah to lie upon him.

On seeing the Rock, Zerah's heart shook as though there were thunder inside it, turning sight into motion. He couldn't tell whether it had aligned some of the disorder in his heart or made it worse. Lightning lit up all the dark places within him. A cry like a newly hatched bird, in awe at seeing life for the very first time, escaped from his lips. The Rock's call to him reached his heart.

But just as Zerah had done with the patch of earth, the cloud, the rain shower, the puddle, and the birdsong, he stopped and remembered his dream.

How much love have I already missed because I'm not yet the Greatest Tree? If I stay, I'll miss even more.

So he journeyed on.

Finally, Zerah reached the top of the mountain. His latest traveling companion, yet another bird, set him down on the highest peak of silver snow so Zerah could see the world. Yet all he could see was fog. Then, through a small opening that reached all the way down to the earth, Zerah saw the Valley.

"Mountaintop!" Zerah called out. "I am Zerah, a seed who needs to know where to root himself! I was told that when I reached you, I would see the world. Yet all I see is fog. Show me the world!"

The Mountaintop laughed. "I am the Mountaintop, not the Fog. Speak to the Fog and ask him to dissipate."

Zerah spoke to the Fog. "Fog! I am Zerah, a seed who needs to know where to root himself! I was told that from the Mountaintop I would see the world, but you are blocking my view. Please clear away!"

The Fog laughed. "I am the Fog, not the Sun. Speak to the Sun and ask him to burn brighter. Then I shall disperse."

Zerah spoke to the Sun. "Sun! I am Zerah, a seed who needs to know where to root himself! I was told that from the Mountaintop I would see the world. But the Fog is blocking my view, and only you can clear him away. Please burn brighter!"

The Sun laughed. "I am the Sun, not the Clouds. Tell the Clouds to move on and my light will shine."

Zerah spoke to the Clouds. "Clouds! I am Zerah, a seed who needs to know where to root himself! I was told that from the Mountaintop I would see the world. But the Fog is blocking my view and only the Sun can clear him away. Yet you are blocking the Sun's light. Please move!"

The Clouds laughed. "We are the Clouds, not the Wind. Tell the Wind to blow and we will move."

"But, but, but," Zerah stuttered.

He did his best to explain to the Clouds that they could move without the Wind, but the Clouds didn't understand how anyone could do anything without the Wind.

For the first time since being crushed, Zerah addressed the Wind. *"Wind! Do you hear me? Move!"*

The Wind did not move.

Zerah screamed louder. *"Didn't you hear me, Wind? I said move!"*

The Wind did not move. Zerah inhaled as deeply as he could. Then, as he exhaled, he cried out with all the strength inside him:

"WIND!"

He took another deep breath before roaring:

"MOOOOOOOOOOOOOVE!"

The breath that had carried Zerah's words out into the world of sound set in motion a single snowflake beneath him. That single snowflake brushed up against another. Two snowflakes shaking caused a third to jostle a fourth. Soon, small clumps of snowflakes were falling off the Mountaintop; miniature shooting stars leaving a trail of silver behind them, stretched long by the Wind, that had returned.

The Wind blew the Clouds out of the Sun's path. As Zerah's body shook atop a collection of trembling snowflakes, who were unsure whether to fall or stay frozen where they were, the Wind made their decision for them. It blew half of them, along with Zerah, off the Mountaintop. Zerah's root and another piece of his body broke off as he fell, frozen in the snow that remained on the Mountaintop.

"Nooooooooooooooo!!" Zerah cried out. *"Wind, don't!"*

But it was already done.

The Wind blew Zerah to the left and right, then further and further away from the mountains. It swirled him in giant circles across the sky. Specks of dust zig-zagged in front of his eyes, and moments of his life flashed through his mind faster than lightning in the sky: a blur of grains of sand, blades of grass, specks of soil, ants, and

birds. The Uprooted Tree. The Little Tree. The Twig. The Sidewalk. The Valley. The Mountaintop. Seeds shaking beside him on his Great Tree. A single seed falling with him. His Great Tree standing tall, giving so much, and loved by so many. And Zerah, doing nothing, having nothing, becoming nothing.

Is this a life? Is this my life? Is this all?

The Wind blew harder, and Zerah fell faster.

He saw tremendous savagery and indescribable beauty. He heard questions he couldn't answer. He felt the pain in his past. He understood that he would feel nothing in his future, for he had no future. It was over.

Grief flooded Zerah's heart, and the Wind, blowing with enough strength to uproot one hundred trees, plunged him into the deep, deep water beneath him. A wave took hold of Zerah and carried him to the surface. Choking, coughing, and gasping for air, he looked around him.

There was no land. There was no hope.

Zerah looked above him. He saw the same sky that had always been; the sky that was home to the sun, moon, and stars, and to the tree branches that grew tall enough to touch the untouchable; the sky that never slept; the sky that was always watching as some dreams were fulfilled and others drowned.

The specks of soil were wrong. Ultimately, I am all alone.

Zerah began to weep, shedding more tears than he ever had before; more tears than he thought existed in the world. They dropped into the water in which he floated, disappearing as though they had never been. When he had no tears left— when everything inside him felt as dry as land that had never known the rain; land on which seeds withered and died—he spoke to the great expanse above and around him.

"Where am I?"

A voice answered, "You are inside me."

"Who are you?" Zerah asked.

"I am an ocean," said the Ocean. "Who are you?"

Zerah thought about that question. *How many times have I been asked that? How many different answers have I given? And why, when the true answer has always been the same?*

"I am Zerah. I am nothing. Just an insignificant, useless, ordinary, sad, lonely, crushed, broken, rootless, little seed."

He paused and looked around him. *What can I become here? How can I ever make meaning here? What rebirth can happen here?*

"And now my life is at its end, and it has made no difference at all. It hasn't mattered."

Zerah lowered his eyes. The Ocean raised hers and watched her lapping waves, carrying Zerah's tears, holding him.

Then she asked him, "Who am I?"

Zerah looked at the Ocean, confused. "You said you were an ocean."

"And what is that?" she asked.

"Water," Zerah stated.

"Countless drops of water," the Ocean corrected. "More than the stars in the sky. More than all the blades of grass in a field. I exist only because those drops of water do. And some of them now exist only because of you. Your life matters."

Zerah's sorrow formed words that were soft and small. "Offering a few drops of water is nothing."

"Not to the ones who need those drops," she replied.

Zerah's next words were quieter and tinier; so close to inaudible that sound barely recognized them. "Offering a few drops of water is nothing compared with what I could have done. I was supposed to be a Great Tree."

Thunder heard a gentler version of itself when the Ocean spoke, her voice reaching far beyond the waves that encircled him. "Many of the drops of water within me once sounded like you, Zerah. You have no idea what you have done or what you can do. And until you root yourself, you never will."

"Root myself?" Zerah asked, his voice rising in volume.

"Root myself?" he repeated, his voice climbing higher and higher. "What do you think I've spent my life trying to do?"

Zerah's voice was so loud that it reached the top of the Ocean's waves. "I'm surrounded by your countless drops of water! Root myself *where?*"

The Ocean rocked Zerah gently as she spoke. "Inside your own heart."

Crushed; broken; so pained that to be touched by eyes was as excruciating as being stepped on by a foot. That was the state of Zerah's heart. He wondered what the Ocean thought he could root himself to? To sorrow? To anger? To disappointment? To the grief that had swallowed up the life that he would never live, and the love that he would never have?

"Didn't you hear what I said?" Zerah asked the Ocean, his voice shrinking with every word he said. "I had a dream, and now it will never, ever come true. I…"

He paused, thinking of the Twig who had told him that his heart could choose life. He thought of the Blades of Grass who had told him that all beings must choose to struggle.

Then he spoke again, his voice infinitesimal. "I give up."

The Ocean's waves moved up and down as she shook her head. "You must *never* give up on your dream. It can, and *must,* come true, especially as it is such a beautiful dream."

Zerah blinked back the Ocean's water from his eyes, but everything was still unclear.

"How do you know that my dream is beautiful? You don't even know what it is. It's much more than simply rooting myself and becoming a Great Tree."

"Of course it is," smiled the Ocean. "And of course I know what your dream is. I know what *everyone's* dream is."

Zerah's mouth dropped open. "No, you don't. You cannot possibly know what everyone's dream is."

"I certainly can," said the Ocean matter-of-factly. "I can and I do. You see, Zerah, everyone dreams the same dream."

"What are you talking about?" he asked, his voice rising even higher than her waves. His frustration, fury, pain, sorrow, and grief surrendered their individual selves and united to claim the power of rage. Every ache Zerah had, every empty, loveless moment, transformed itself into words to flail upon the Ocean.

"You stupid Ocean! You foolish Ocean! You know-it-all Ocean! What are you talking about? Not all dreams are the same! A grain of sand that dreams of living in a desert is not dreaming the same dream as a grain of sand that dreams of living on an ocean's floor. A branch that dreams of remaining on her tree is not dreaming the same dream as a branch that dreams of climbing a mountain. A bush's dream of wings is not the same as a bee's dream of roots. A bird's dream of flying higher than all others is not the same as a chipmunk's dream of digging deeper than anyone else. Blades of grass that dream of growing are not dreaming the same dream as a sidewalk that dreams of smothering them. A car that dreams of breaking others is not dreaming the same dream as a twig that dreams of helping others become whole. You dumb Ocean! You crazy Ocean! How are these dreams the same?"

The Ocean's waves crashed down, sending drops of water soaring skywards. Then back into the Ocean those drops fell, part of the great whole once more.

When she spoke, her voice sounded like the music Zerah had once heard while growing on his Great Tree: a song he had hoped to have the power to sing one day.

"But of course they are the same dream. It is *always* the same dream. It is the dream of being important, useful, special, happy, and, most of all, loved. A grain of sand that dreams of living forever in a desert… does she dream this because she hates the desert? Or because she loves the desert and feels love in return? A grain of sand that dreams of living on an ocean's floor… does he dream this because he loves an ocean? Or because he doesn't feel love where he is and believes that, in another time and place, he will? A branch that feels important growing on a tree, offering shade and a place to rest, and a branch that finds her use in climbing a mountain, in offering help to continue walking: which is not dreaming of living a life that matters? Is a bush dreaming of wings seeking misery or happiness? Does a bee dream of roots because she wants to wander forever, or to be forever at home, and forever embraced?

Does a bird dream of flying higher than all others and a chipmunk dream of digging deeper than anyone else because they want to be special or ordinary? Are blades of grass that dream of the sky seeking pain, or freedom and joy? Does a twig dream of helping others because she hates them? Or because she loves them and wants their own dreams to come true?

"And what of a sidewalk that dreams of smothering and a car that dreams of breaking? Those are not dreams. Those are nightmares born of the savage belief that no life has worth, not even one's own. For who would fill their days and nights with acts of savagery except one who does not value those days and nights enough to fill them with beauty? Who would misuse and waste their own life so tragically, save for one who finds no worth in it?

"And what of those who do not dream? There is no such thing. There is slumber, but all who sleep can be awakened, and the dream they dream can be fulfilled. The dream is *love*. That is how I know what your dream is. Because it is *everyone's* dream. And that is how I know it is beautiful, because there is nothing more beautiful than the dream of love."

The Ocean fell silent for a moment, and Zerah remained quiet inside her.

Then he spoke softly. "You are right. I dreamed of love. And I dreamed of being important and useful and special and happy. I dreamed that becoming a Great Tree would give me these things and make me these things. But I cannot become a Great Tree inside an Ocean. I cannot become a tree at all."

The Ocean gazed tenderly upon him, then said, "Seeds are not to be loved for who they can become, but for who they already are."

The stars recognized their own light in her words, but Zerah saw nothing to illumine the darkness he was lost within. He lowered his eyes and saw his reflection in the drops of water below him, united as one. He quickly turned away.

"It is trees who are loved for who they are, not seeds."

"The stars refuse no one light," she responded. "Drops of water treat every throat and eye with the same dignity. The earth rejects no one's body. The sky never has, and never will, turn its face from anyone. They all love trees, just like seeds, simply because they are. But I, who exist only because the essence of the drops of water never changes, feel differently. Choice is what matters most to me. I do not love trees for who they choose to become, but for who they choose to remain."

Remain, Zerah thought. *The Valley asked the same thing of me. Who would I be if I had remained in the Valley? Perhaps my body would not have been broken again, but my heart still wouldn't be whole. Who would I be if I had remained on my Great Tree?*

He saw himself as a little seed: whole in body but with an empty heart. He was looking into the distant, uncertain future with a faith so strong that distance felt like tomorrow and uncertainty felt sure.

Remain, Zerah thought again. He saw his life before he had known what his life was supposed to be; what he was expected to achieve. He saw himself swinging beside Semeeya in the sunlight, surrounded by gold. Sometimes it burned, but he never felt like he was facing the fire alone. He saw the moon, forever changing, forever remaining the same. He saw the stars in the sky, and he heard himself say "Wow!" and "Why?" so many times that wonder became as constant as breathing.

He had not yet seen savagery. The Wind had not yet been named. Rain poured down on his body. Mist sometimes accompanied the sun and moon to wakefulness and sleep, but everything was clear. Semeeya was beside him laughing, offering kindness and love. He was simply returning it. That had been enough to make him great in her eyes, and enough for him to see greatness in her.

Zerah had felt no need to search for a home. He had experienced one in that feeling of total acceptance, where nothing burned or drowned; where the body sought rest, light, and water, but the heart was continually restored without seeking, and beauty needed no confirmation. Being remembered by other seeds or trees or animals or humans or insects hadn't been important. The kindness and love in each moment had. He hadn't needed to prove to himself or anyone else that he mattered. He had known that he did.

And then he had accepted two teachings without even being aware that he was doing so. These teachings had been given with the same lack of awareness; offered not only by his Great Tree, but by the other Great Trees growing beside his own, as well as those growing in the fields in the distance. Sometimes their voices were loud and mighty; at other times they were soft echoes which belied the power of their source. The teachings they offered became beliefs.

"You will be loved when…" The conditions following that "when" had not always been the same. The height of the trunk, the thickness of the branches, the size of the leaves, the shape of the fruit, the color of the flowers, and the number of future seeds growing on a future tree varied. But the existence of a condition did not, and neither did that condition's effect. Doubting a Great Tree's love left a seed doubting others' love and their sense of worthiness.

"You will be great when…" It was a vision of the future that silenced the song and stilled the dance of the present. It was a vision that bore and buried dreams with the same breath; a vision that stripped journeys and beings of what made them so beautiful: difference. Nevertheless, it was a vision that held one's gaze like a flower held a bee's heart. It was too sweet to turn away from.

How many hurtful teachings exist? Zerah wondered. *With teachers like the stars, how could the teachings "loved when" and "great when" ever be taught to a seed? With teachers like the stars, how could a seed ever believe the teachings "loved when" and "great when"? With the truth of love, how can any beliefs that don't reflect it exist? And why is it still so difficult to believe the truth?*

Having lived outside his own heart for so long, Zerah didn't know his way back into it, or even if there was room for him. He had once thought his heart was empty. Now he understood that his heart had always been full; once with love and an understanding of what greatness truly was, and now with so many feelings that he didn't want. Yet he didn't know how to be rid of them. Zerah soon found himself wondering whether he had remained or changed.

Zerah spoke to the Ocean, his eyes lowered, his face flushed. "If someone has a heart full of feelings—not only love and kindness—does that heart belong to one who has changed, or to one who has remained?"

The Ocean held Zerah gently within her waves and said, "That heart belongs to one who lives."

She paused for a moment before continuing. "We can change and still remain. Drops of water do it every moment of every day. We can feel many things and still fill our days and nights with noble choices. That may be a struggle, but in this act of struggling, we remain. To exert power over your heart, instead of someone else's life, is to remain. To die and be reborn and not forsake your dream is to remain. To offer an ocean tears filled with a longing for love—tears that can change and embrace a seed—is to change and to remain."

Silence engulfed Zerah while he thought about the Ocean's words. They did what many words, both helpful and hurtful, do: they made the trek from the head down into the heart and settled inside it. Then they did what only beautiful words can do: they stood like mirrors before the word *miracle*, reflecting its truth in many directions. They became the music notes that words should be. They hummed the melody of the song Zerah had one day hoped to sing: *"I am loved."*

When a long rest interrupted that music, Zerah saw beyond his present into the future. It was hazier than it had ever been before, and filled with many choices. He heard the words of the Crack in the Sidewalk speaking a truth he was afraid to hear: "Knowing who someone is in the present doesn't necessarily tell you who they will become in the future."

What if one day I change, but do not remain? Zerah wondered.

Then he remembered that the Third Blade of Grass had already answered that question: return to who he once was.

Zerah asked the Ocean, "Can I stay with you a while?"

The Ocean answered, "For as long as you want." She smiled at Zerah, and then the soft sound of lapping waves filled up his ears as her voice had done a moment ago.

Zerah looked up into the sky. The clouds passing overhead opened like a heart that was unafraid to share what was inside it. Raindrops poured down, their straight path turned diagonally, sideways, and even upside down by the Wind before they eventually fell into the Ocean's waves.

Drops of water colliding with other drops of water sang a song of union that accompanied their change: rain to wave, wave to foam, foam to mist, and back again;

silver shedding white, swallowing blue, and relinquishing color, only to absorb it once more. It was a constant cycle of transformation, and yet the drops' essence always remained the same. And because they did, so did the Ocean. Her waves continued to rise and fall, and she continued to hold Zerah, as well as everything else inside her, in a gentle embrace.

For many sunrises and sunsets, Zerah floated in the Ocean. The waves carried him skyward and then brought him back down. Meanwhile, moments from his life passed through his mind once again. But this time, they didn't flash like lightning. They crawled like the Snail. And like the Rabbit with insatiable eyes, it didn't matter how much they consumed. It was never enough. There was always more to see.

Like the Snake who journeyed backward, Zerah traveled back down the mountain in his mind. He saw some of the love he had missed—not because he hadn't become a Great Tree, but because he had believed that he needed to become one.

He saw conversations begun and ended in the same breath.

He saw a dragonfly offering friendship, and he saw himself, unaware that friendship was being offered.

The purple patch of earth, cloud, rain shower, puddle, and birdsong dug holes in his heart; in the places where sweet memories might have been. On the rock lay a single question: *What if?* The Twig had told Zerah not to ask it, but he couldn't stop asking.

Zerah saw some of the love others had missed because he hadn't offered his love. Then he heard it. There was the Rock, his heart breaking, a quiet cry marking the change, when his question to Zerah—"Will you stay with me?"—had been answered with, "I have to go." There was the tender voice of a single grain of sand pushed low into hurt and pulled high into anger.

Beneath the Mountaintop was the Valley with an offer of truth on his lips. Zerah had forsaken it for a belief.

Zerah saw the love everyone had missed. The love that did not exist. The struggles that should never have been. The void where all meaning was gone, because savage teachings were taught and believed, and because savage choices were made. Because power was feared and lives were not valued. Because some became, but they did not remain.

Zerah saw the love he had sought: animals crowding around him, humans praising him, insects bowing down to him. This love was supposed to make him whole by filling all the places where he felt something missing: the Wind absent, his Great Tree out of reach, the Twig, blades of grass, specks of soil, and ants far behind him, Semeeya even further, he not inside his own heart.

Then Zerah saw himself as he was. At first it was hard to look. The first thing he had seen in the desert and the city, then in the Valley, on the Mountaintop, and in the Ocean, had been lack. When he looked at his life, he saw the same lack. In the brief moments when the waves were still and his reflection was everywhere, that lack was multiplied many times over: a hundred jagged edges instead of one, each shedding tears for the roots they would never have. A hundred missing trunks, a thousand missing branches, absent leaves outlining a future as dark as a starless sky. Unyielding hunger. Inalterable ugliness. Grief for the death of his seeds; seeds that had never even lived. He shed tears again.

The waves continued to rise and fall. His feelings soared and sank as though they were tied to the crashing waves. Everything he had felt, and everything he had been afraid to feel, was there waiting for him; waiting for its turn to be recognized and heard. Confusion, mass confusion, soon arose because multiple feelings attached themselves to everyone he knew, and every experience he had had; to every choice he had chosen, and every choice he had not.

Then Zerah—who had searched so long for a place to root himself and hold fast to—did just the opposite. He let go. He let go of his beliefs: of who he was supposed to be; what he was supposed to have and do; where he was supposed to root himself; and how he was supposed to feel. Into the Ocean he shed the invisible that had borne the visible into being. Layers of an imagined life peeled away from his heart, and he accepted what remained beneath them: his past, his present, and himself, just as he was, with his broken body, broken heart, and uncomprehending mind.

Not a single drop of water, or even every droplet filling up the Ocean, could have prepared Zerah for what happened next. When he accepted himself as he was, he began to change. A crushed seed, too weak and small to prevent pain and injustice, became a powerful seed, not only strong enough to survive being crushed, but strong enough to survive a deep, dark hole, two falls, a break, and a near drowning. As he thought of the injustice in the world, he wondered, *What else am I powerful enough to do?*

Zerah's jealousy became a hunger to know others' stories. His bitterness became compassion, as he already knew some of those stories. A lonely seed found constant companionship, not only from the sky, but from those who flew within it, as well as those who walked, crawled and swam beneath it, struggling to fulfill their dreams and remain when savagery, pain, and injustice tried desperately to convince their love and kindness to go away.

A heart filled with anger, pain, and sorrow became a heart brave enough to experience those feelings. Then his heart bowed down to his mind so he could figure out what to do with all that anger, pain, and sorrow.

A seed full of fear faced what scared him most: the belief that neither his joy nor his pain mattered; that his entire life was inconsequential; that he himself was nothing.

When Zerah looked again, he saw something that had remained hidden behind the massive shadow of an imaginary tree; something that he had forsaken, though it had never forsaken him; something he had deemed small. In fact, it was boundless. He saw the tremendous love he had been given and the tremendous love he had given in return. It was love that broke and love that healed; imperfect love and unspoken love, but love nonetheless.

The synonym of this love was not *praise*, but *listen, help, carry, hold, smile,* and *hope.* It was love that often went unnoticed, not recognized for what it was; given and received in near silence, disappearing into that quiet as though it had never been. But it had been, and it still was. It moved within Zerah. Truth battled belief, and truth eventually won. Zerah finally understood that, like every single drop of water, he mattered.

Then one more struggle that should never have been was over as Zerah found himself, just as he was, living inside his own heart, held in place by a single, tiny, sturdy
root.

"There is nothing more beautiful than the dream of love," the Ocean had told him.

Zerah raised his eyes, looked at his reflection in the Ocean, and told her, "More
beautiful than the dream of love is the dream of love fulfilled."

The Ocean nodded her head. Her waves were calm now, and the ripples they made
were small. But each one was so consistent, so persistent, that the tears of joy within
them were carried far, far beyond what Zerah could see.

A SINGLE TEAR dropped into the Ocean beside Zerah one day, disappearing into the waves almost as though it had never been. But it had been, and Zerah and the Ocean had seen it.

Zerah didn't know whose eye had shed the tear, but having watched it disappear into a wave, he said to the Ocean, "I don't know why, but my heart is telling me that it's time to go."

The Ocean looked at Zerah and smiled. "Then it must indeed be time."

Zerah smiled back. He felt her waves, which had long held him, beginning to carry him towards… he didn't know what. If they had a destination in mind, they didn't share it, and Zerah didn't ask about it. He was empty; not of love, but of plans. Only the journey was left.

With his eyes opened as wide as his heart, Zerah looked at those around him and listened to their stories. Some drops of water had risen from the depths to see the sun and tell the story of darkness.

"Sometimes it's hard to stop seeing the dark, even when you're surrounded by light," one said.

Others had fallen from the sky to seek out a land made of water and to recount the lessons of a life lived too close to the sun.

"With so much light, it's almost impossible to see clearly," explained another.

Zerah also listened to the stories of those who floated beside him in the Ocean, telling their tales of changed plans, long journeys, and dreams fulfilled.

The waves soon carried Zerah to a shore. He kissed the Ocean goodbye and she kissed him back. Just before the last wave receded, Zerah said to himself, "Stay with me." "OK," he replied. No reasons were needed.

Zerah looked around him. The first thing he saw was abundance: countless grains of sand.

He started to speak to one. "Hello, I'm—"

The Wind stirred beside Zerah and picked him up. It carried him far beyond the shore and deposited him upon a small, reddish-brown patch of earth. Zerah heard a voice speaking.

"Someday, little seeds, you will become Great Trees. When it is time for you to drop, the Wind will carry you to a field where you will root yourselves and grow trunks, branches, leaves, fruit, flowers, and seeds of your own. Once you have grown these things, you will do great things. You will house the homeless, give rest to the tired, satiate the hungry, add beauty to the world, and ensure your eternal life. Then you will be important, useful, and special. Your life will matter. And you will be happy."

Zerah looked up. Before him stood a tree, and growing on her branches were hundreds of seeds. They were nodding their heads and speaking the words, "I will be." The seeds smiled as a single tear appeared in each pair of eyes.

Suddenly, Zerah heard his own voice. "No!" he shouted. "You *are*!"

"Did someone say something?" asked the Tree.

"I did!" Zerah shouted again.

"Who are you?" asked the Tree. And then, as she surveyed the space around her, she asked, "Where are you?"

"Down here!" Zerah hollered.

The Tree looked down. Beneath her sat a little seed.

"Who are you?" the Tree asked again.

"I am Zerah," he said.

"Well, Zerah, I am—"

Zerah cut the Tree off. "I know who you are. You are a tree."

The Tree frowned. "You mean a Great Tree! And these are my seeds, all of whom will become Great Trees themselves one day."

"And what if they don't?" he asked.

The Tree and all the little seeds gasped.

"Uhhh! Wind forbid it!" cried the Tree. "Not become a Great Tree? Why, who ever heard of a seed not becoming a Great Tree?" Then she took another look at Zerah. "Ohhh," she said with pity in her voice. And then again, "Ohhh," with the slightest chuckle.

"You know," Zerah said to the seeds, "you don't need to wait to add beauty. Your existence already does that. You don't need a trunk or branches or leaves or fruit or flowers or seeds of your own to be important, useful, special, or happy, or to have a life that matters. Your life matters now. And although housing, providing rest, and feeding are great things, you don't need to do them to be great."

Zerah paused as he thought of the words he had offered the First Grain of Sand, the human who had wanted to turn the desert into a city, and the Sidewalk who had considered himself great. He recalled the Valley's rhyme, which he finally understood.

Then he added, "In fact, if you have all the things a tree has but do not have what is most essential, if you do all that you are planning to do but without what is most vital, your houses will be unstable and your shade only partial. Your words will break. Your actions will crush. Your rest will be nonexistent, your fruit bitter, your beauty superficial, and your seeds unaware of their own *and* others' worth."

There was silence for a moment. The little seeds looked at the Tree, then at Zerah. The Tree looked at her seeds, then at Zerah. Her face flushed red and gold, like a fire in its early stages. Her laughter, rising high and spreading fast, promised to burn. Soon, all but one of the little seeds echoed that laughter.

"Spoken like a seed who *has nothing* and *has done nothing* with his life. Spoken like a seed who *is nothing*." The Tree looked at her little seeds again, then back at Zerah. "Take a good look, little seeds, at Zerah. Everyone and everything in this world has something to teach, and Zerah here can teach you who *not* to be. I mean, who are *you* to speak of greatness? Who are you, Zerah, but a little, insignificant, useless, ordinary seed?

"And you are not only those things. You are crushed. You are broken. You are sopping wet, dripping water everywhere. No wonder you have been unable to root yourself. I imagine the ground would not want a seed like *you* growing inside it. Nor,

I'm sure, would anyone want to root themselves beside your sad, lonely self. Tell me, trunkless Zerah, branchless Zerah, leafless Zerah, fruitless Zerah, flowerless Zerah, barren Zerah, all but invisible and soon-to-be forgotten Zerah, what do you have? And you, who do not, who *cannot* offer what I do to the world, what do you offer? What do you *do?*"

The Tree glared at Zerah, and the little seeds followed suit.

Zerah looked inside his own heart. The words of the Tree felt like a windstorm, beating down on the seed of love that had taken root inside his heart and grown into a tree of love.

The tree swayed.

The tree shook.

But the tree was not uprooted.

Zerah smiled. "I have love," he told the Tree and the little seeds. "And what I choose to do with it," he paused for a moment before saying, "is offer it to you."

"*Love?*" asked the Tree. "What is that?"

Zerah beheld the Tree before him, but thoughts of his own Great Tree filled his mind. Then an ache filled his heart.

Now I understand why trees teach seeds, "You will be loved when…" and "You will be great when…" It is because they believe it themselves. It is because they, too, are dreaming of love. It is because they, too, doubt their own worthiness of love. So much so that perhaps they, like seeds, cannot always recognize love. Is it fear that created these teachings? Why are we all so afraid?

It was then that Zerah clearly heard the voices of animals, humans, and insects accompanying the trees, intoning the same sad refrain of "*loved when…*" and "*great when…*", their legs and wings straining, aching; reaching out for something that was already within reach.

Zerah looked back at his life. He realized that of all the things he might be, broken was no longer one of them.

He spoke to the Tree. "'What is love?' you ask. Love is one seed on a branch following another seed as they fall into the Wind together. Love is a grain of sand offering her time and filling it with concern. Love is another grain of sand revealing the space in his heart where a forsaken but not forgotten dream still dwells. Love is a little tree's faith in goodness. Love is numerous grains of sand sharing all the knowledge they have. Love is a twig sitting day after day in the dark with a seed until the seed sees the light.

"Love is blades of grass who refuse to give up. Love is specks of soil living side by side.

"Love is ants carrying a seed out of a deep, dark hole, and a bird carrying a seed up into the sky. Love is a valley who can always see depth. Love is a rock appreciating the beauty in a seed even when the seed cannot see it in himself.

"Love is drops of water remaining the same. Love is an ocean who changes. Love is the earth embracing humans' feet and the sky embracing birds' wings.

"Love is seeds wanting to make a tree proud. And love is a tree wanting to be loved."

The Tree remained silent for a moment. She lowered her eyes, then raised them to find all her seeds looking up at her. She bristled under their gaze, then released peals of laughter, long and harsh. All but two of the little seeds laughed with her.

"As I was saying, little seeds, some will teach you who to be, and others who not to be. Just make sure you know the difference."

All but three of the little seeds nodded their heads in agreement.

Just then, a breeze came along. It rattled the branches and leaves and seeds. It encircled Zerah, lifting him high off the ground, and carried him away from the Tree.

But right before it did, Zerah heard four voices say, "Love is seeds loving themselves, not because of what they have or do, but just because they are."

 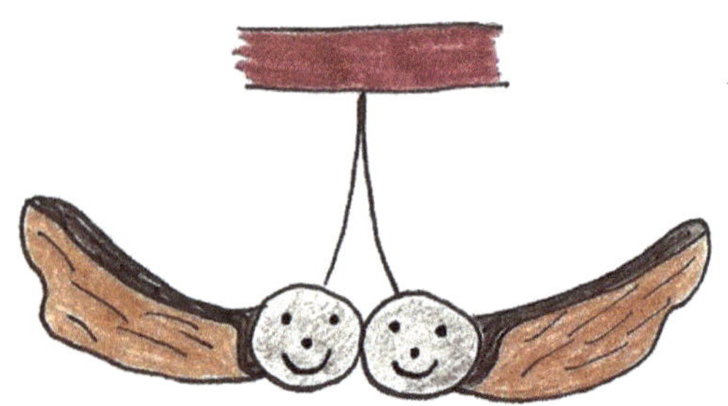

Enveloped by the Wind again, Zerah looked into *its* heart for the very first time. He was certain that the Twig was right; that all beings had a heart. The fact that the heart might be filled with anger or pain or fear didn't mean it was absent. Neither did it mean that these were the only feelings within that heart.

"Wind?" Zerah asked. "Are you afraid that your life doesn't matter? Are you afraid that if you don't uproot trees and blow seeds into deserts, no one will know you exist? Is that why your little breezes become tornadoes and your drafts hurricanes? Are you afraid to look inside your own heart? Are you afraid of all that dwells there? Are you dreaming of love? Or are you trying to spread that dream and fulfill it? Or…are you? Just that—you simply are."

The Wind was still for a moment. Then it continued to blow, rattling and caressing seeds, trees, animals, humans, and insects with one tremendous, solitary breath. Encircled by it, Zerah continued to whirl through the sky.

Zerah did not become a tree... He could not become a tree. He was nibbled at by a hungry mouse, and after that it simply wasn't possible for him to take root in the soil. But Zerah remained who he was. Love, rooted in his heart, remained where it was. And the questions the blades of grass had told Zerah he must answer also remained, waiting for his answers.

Many of those questions could not be answered by him alone, for it is not the place of a single seed to decree the fate of many. But one of those questions could only be answered in the quiet of Zerah's own heart: *How can I make meaning?*

Yet it was not Zerah's heart that answered first, but his mind. *Feelings,* his mind said. *Feelings,* his heart repeated.

The more Zerah thought about feelings, the more it seemed silly, strange, sad, tragic, horrific, and absurd that so many struggles that should never have been—so much savagery, injustice, and pain—had been conceived by one solitary feeling: fear. Fear that had created teachings, which had birthed beliefs, which had been the causes of, but not the justifications for, savage choices. Fear that had grown and grown until it had turned into colossal, cursed trees, large enough to block out the light of the stars, with limbs like thorns and fruit like poison. Fear that had rooted itself to hearts and severed their connection to minds, where truths also dwell, so that if either the head or the heart forgot, the other could remind it. Fear that was trying desperately to maintain its death grip upon hope.

How can I make meaning? Zerah asked himself again. He thought of everything he could possibly choose and remembered that love was indeed among the choices. *I will offer another feeling: love. I will do what so many have done for me. I will help make others' dreams come true.*

And so the journey continued. Zerah's traveling companions were as plentiful as the stars in the sky. On ants' backs, tucked under birds' wings, gently held inside puppies' paws, and still whirling inside the Wind, Zerah moved through the world. His eyes shared some of the sky's knowledge as he returned to places he had already been and travelled to new ones: farms and forests, glaciers and gardens, jungles and caves, rivers and reefs, plains and parks. In exchange for legs and wings, Zerah offered his traveling companions his ear, his time, and a space inside his heart. He heard words and witnessed lives in the same way the Ocean welcomed drops of water: with the understanding that every single one mattered.

And after Zerah listened, he spoke; or rather he sang. It wasn't the song he had long wanted to sing, but one that was much more beautiful; one that others had taught him to sing:

> *You are the same as me:*
> *important, useful, special, and loved.*
> *With an open heart you can clearly see.*
> *The grains of sand to our left,*
> *the blades of grass to our right,*
> *the ants that crawl,*
> *the birds in flight,*
> *the trees behind us,*
> *the seeds before us,*
> *the ground below us,*
> *the sky above us,*
> *the animals, humans, and insects all around us.*
> *This truth every single one of us shares:*
> *your life matters,*
> *and so does theirs.*

As Zerah journeyed on, the sun set and rose, forever fulfilling his promise to the night: "I will return." The moon waxed and waned, speaking of eternity and telling old tales about that which would never change: the existence of love. The there and yesterday, here and now, near and soon, far and later, and beyond and one day heard the same melody; at times quiet, at others loud, but never unsung. A mad dance carried on, with seeds, drops of water, and specks of dust whirling inside the Wind, colliding with one another. The terrified, jagged rocks spinning beside them howled, "There is no choice," while a chorus led by a grain of sand, a twig, five blades of grass, countless specks of soil, a valley, an ocean, and a seed named Zerah sang of choice.

And in that choice, there is hope.

One day, when Zerah was very, very old, the Wind deposited him beside the roots of a very, very great tree. As Zerah gazed up at her, a sweet, tender, and familiar voice spoke his name.

"Zerah? Is that you?"

Zerah stared at the tree before him. "Semeeya?"

"Zerah!" cried Semeeya. "It *is* you! I can't believe it. I almost didn't recognize you. You've grown so much!"

Zerah wept and laughed all at once.

"Me? Look at you! You're enormous!"

A squirrel carried Zerah up into Semeeya's branches. She hugged him tightly with her leaves.

They remained in that embrace for a long time, so close that not even a single word found space to be voiced. But once their embrace loosened, a river of speech began to flow, which could not be stopped.

"It feels like it was in another life," Semeeya began, "that day when the Wind carried you off, replacing the companionship I thought we would always have with questions that hurt to ask and were impossible to answer. Where were you? Why did the Wind take you? When would it bring you back? What if you never came back? How could I find you? I watered the soil around me with my tears, and I soon began to sink into the earth. Then hope, which had left me, returned. I thought that if I could grow tall enough, I would be able to see wherever you were.

"The soil made a place for me right away. Growing my first root was so easy, but

ZERAH

nothing else was. Many days and nights passed without rain. Some creatures starved. Then there were floods, and other creatures drowned. I asked why many times over, but I still don't have any answers."

A tear fell from Semeeya's eye, and a parched ant beneath her quenched his thirst. Zerah kissed one of Semeeya's branches. She smiled, took a deep breath, and spoke again.

"Others died, but I survived. I began to grow taller and wider. My trunk shot up and my branches stretched far beyond it. My roots dug deep into the earth, and all the nutrients the soil shared with me, I shared with the leaves I had begun to grow. Yet no matter how much nourishment I was given, and no matter how much I gave, I couldn't grow the tremendous orange fruit and flowers the colors of the evening sky our Great Tree told me I would. I thought there was something wrong with me. It took me many, many sunrises and sunsets to realize that our Great Tree never had these things either. It was the trees next to him who had them."

Zerah closed his eyes to recall memories of their Great Tree. When he found them, he discovered that Semeeya was right.

Then another sleeping memory opened like a flower in the light of the sun. The tree he had met after leaving the Ocean had also been missing the fruit and flowers she had told her seeds they would grow.

Zerah shook his head and said, "How different life might be if kindness were a measure of achievement."

Semeeya smiled. "How different indeed."

She gazed up at the sky and wondered what it would be like to see everything the sky had seen: countless days and nights filled with kindness and savagery. And then one day, after all those sunsets and sunrises, to see only kindness. What color would the sky be then? She stared for a moment longer before turning back to Zerah and resuming her story.

"Though I couldn't grow fruit or flowers, I continued to grow. I kept looking for you, but I still couldn't see you. And then my life changed, and I could only look back at a past that was gone; not at a present that was, or into a future that felt like it

would never be.

"As a seed, I thought frozen was something that only happened to your body. But when the first leaves I'd ever grown began to fall, crumbling into the earth below me as though they had never been, yet still singing, dancing, and laughing inside my heart, my joy froze within me. Frost covered a garden full of buds that I thought would never bloom. I became winter itself. I understood the horrific pain of a beautiful truth: that love outlives death. But truth doesn't always bring comfort."

Another tear fell from Semeeya's eye, and a mouse received a reprieve from the sun's heat.

Zerah nodded in agreement. "It depends on the truth." Then he thought of the teachings *"loved when"* and *"great when"* and wondered whether it wasn't easier to believe them than the truth of love, but simply less painful. It hurt less to feel only his own sorrow rather than that of his Great Tree; of his beloved Great Tree.

"But life goes on," Semeeya said, "whether we find comfort in truth or pain. Our choice is whether to go on with it or not."

"Are you glad you did?" asked Zerah.

Semeeya nodded. "I wasn't then, but I am now."

"That's why hope is so important," said Zerah.

"And faith," Semeeya added.

"In the Wind?" Zerah asked.

"In tomorrow. And in the knowledge that it can be better than today."

The leaves that had once grown on Semeeya's branches stirred inside her heart, mixing love and pain so thoroughly that at times they felt like one emotion. Then the new leaves on her branches rustled in the Wind, swinging back and forth, smiling, and asking her to continue the story.

"Soon new leaves formed. Life seeks life. Birds built nests in my branches, humans rested beneath me, and ants crawled over me. Praise filled my ears, and the sense of purpose that had once been a plan became a way of life.

"Then one winter I became very sick. One piece of bark after another peeled off me until nothing was left. My leaves fell, but new ones did not grow. My branches turned gray. Parts of them broke even when no one and nothing touched them. A human came and cut off what was left. Once my bark and branches were gone, the animals, humans, and insects did not return. I learned that need is not the same thing as love. And in their absence, I found that listening, not speaking, was what I craved the most. I didn't miss their words of praise, but I longed for my pain to be heard; not only by the ground and the sky, but by those who shared life with me on the same ground and beneath the same sky." Semeeya paused for a moment, then added, "How different life might be if listening were a measure of achievement."

Zerah said, "Then success would be measured by whose conversations lasted the longest, whose understanding grew the most, and whose heart opened the widest."

Semeeya smiled. "But if it were so, there would be no measurements at all."

She looked up at the sky and wondered for a moment what it might be like to see all the frenetic movement become still, and hear nothing but the sound of stories being told and the silence of stories being heard.

"For a very long time, every sunrise was accompanied by the thought of what I could do if only I still had my bark, limbs and leaves, and every sunset took with it another day wasted, full of moments as numerous as the blades of grass in a field; moments that could have been filled with *I am* and *I can* and *I did* instead of *if only*.

"Then one day, two humans—two very little yet very great ones—came to visit me. They returned every day and stayed so long that my memories of love began to multiply. Those memories kept me company in the evenings when the little humans were gone, and the ache of lost bark, branches and leaves was present. The little humans didn't care that I wasn't a great tree, but they did care about me. They gave me their ears, their time, and a space inside their hearts. With their offerings of unconditional love, I began to get well.

"The impossible is possible. My bark and branches grew again. New leaves unfurled the surprise of chartreuse and dark green sharing space with emerald. Animals, humans, and insects flocked to me. At first I was angry. Where had they been when I was sick? But when they told me about their own illnesses, their own pains, and their own struggles, empathy grew within me. I decided to offer them all I had.

"But that wasn't enough. My trunk was too thin, my branches too few, my leaves too small to house and shade all that I wanted to. Nothing I had was good enough. Nothing I did was great enough.

"It was in that moment that I grew seeds for the first time. I thought their lives were mine. I was wrong. I thought they were voiceless, and that it was my place to speak for them. I was wrong. No one and nothing is without a voice. No one and nothing needs to be spoken for. They only need to be listened to.

"I did not listen to my seeds. I sent them into the world with instructions to become great trees and do all that I had been unable to do. I became obsessed with what I hadn't done, rather than proud of what I had done. I constantly lamented what I felt I lacked and became jealous of other trees. I didn't know who I was. I *forgot* who I was."

Zerah thought of the Twig. "Knowledge is important," he said, "and so are reminders when we forget it. Who reminded you? The little humans?"

Semeeya smiled. "The little humans grew big one day. They told me they needed to leave in order to pursue and fulfill their dreams. I understood. They were gone for many sunrises and sunsets.

"One night they returned with an object called a mirror in their hands and an offering of a seed in their hearts. They said if I looked into that silver surface, I would know who I was. I looked. With the stars gleaming behind me—too many to ever count—all I saw was light."

Semeeya showed Zerah the mirror leaning up against her trunk, sitting firmly on her roots.

"Look into the mirror," she said. "I'll wait while you do. I know the stars aren't visible now, but if you look closely, you'll see what I saw."

An ant carried Zerah down to the mirror and a butterfly flew him back up into Semeeya's branches.

"From that moment on, I offered the seeds I grew only two teachings: *loved always,* and *always love.*"

They both smiled.

"Well, Zerah," Semeeya beamed at him. "It has been so long, and I have so much more to tell you. But now it's your turn. Tell me about your life!"

Zerah remained silent for a moment. Then he breathed in deeply, exhaled fully, and said, "Where do I begin? Perhaps with the end. Or maybe with the continuation…

"There was once a seed named Zerah. His name will fade, but the love he gave will remain."

Acknowledgments

Were I to name everyone who has given me the greatest offerings one can ever give—their ear, their time, and a space inside their hearts—many pages would follow this one. Were I to list all of those who have taken me out of deep, dark holes and up into the sky, many more pages would need to be added.

However unintentionally, some names fade, yet the love and kindness given remain. Other names are never shared. They belong to the strangers whose paths cross with ours briefly but irrevocably; to the people who are exactly where we need them to be, exactly when we need them to be there.

Still others are not even named: seeds and trees and grains of sand who do their work without accolades and often without acknowledgment, simply because it is upon them to do their tremendous work of teaching beauty and peace.

In an effort to omit no one from the very long list of sacred souls to whom I am grateful, let me simply say:

To my family, friends, students, teachers, healers, helpers; to those who welcomed me into their homes as I wandered the world seeking answers and writing snippets of this story; to those who supported my writing and supported me; to those who had enough faith to make up for my lack of it; to those who wrote, spoke, dreamed of, and worked toward a better world, and to those who continue to do so; to those who answered, "Kindness" in response to the question, "What will you give this stranger before you?"; to the trees and ants that reached me in the moments when no human being could; to my fellow travelers, sharers of fruit and flowers, and struggles and questions and dreams: I bow to you in love and gratitude.

With my whole heart, I thank you.